KID
POWER
STRIKES
BACK

D0377684

KID POWER STRIKES BACK

Susan Beth Pfeffer

Illustrated by Leigh Grant

AN
APPLE
PAPERBACK

SCHOLASTIC INC.
New York Toronto London Auckland Sydney

ISBN 0-590-33468-9

12 11 10 9 8 7 6 5 4 3 2 1   7 8 9/8 0 1 2/9

Printed in the U.S.A.   11

First Scholastic printing, December 1987

For the kids of Middletown

KID
POWER
STRIKES
BACK

Chapter

1

"Smile, Janie!"

"I am smiling," I growled.

"Then smile harder," my mother instructed me. "And don't squint."

"I have to squint," I told her. "The sun's in my eyes."

"Then shield your eyes until I say when," Mom replied. "We want a nice picture of you in front of your new bike."

I sighed, shielded my eyes, smiled, and quickly removed my hand from my face when my mother told me to. She took two quick pictures of me standing by the bike, and then one of the bike without me. "For your scrapbook," she told me when I gave her a weird look. As though I'd want a picture of my bike in my scrapbook. As though I could even remember where my scrapbook was anymore.

My mother had bought the kind of camera that develops the pictures itself, so in a minute, I was looking at three pictures of me and my bike. In one of them I was definitely squinting, but the others came out okay.

"This camera was such a great idea," my mother said. "It'll give that something extra to Something Extra."

I sighed some more. My mother had taken to saying that about practically everything lately. "It's getting cold, Mom," I said. "Mind if I go in?"

"Not at all," my mother said. "Just put your bike away first."

So I moved it into the garage. It was a beautiful bike, and I wasn't really sure why it didn't make me happier. I'd earned half the money for it myself, by working all summer for my organization, Kid Power. I'd created Kid Power just to earn the money for the bike, and while I'd been working and saving, it had been fun to have a goal. But the time finally came when I had enough money, and a little extra to keep my savings account open. My mother really started after me then about when I was going to buy the bike, so I finally gave in, withdrew the money, and went bike shopping with her that morning. And now I had my bike, and there wasn't any reason to even pretend Kid Power still existed.

I kicked at some leaves on the driveway as I walked back to the house. There hadn't been much time for Kid Power anyway once school started. At its peak, in August, I had three of my friends, plus my sister Carol and me all working for it. I put all of the money I earned into my savings account, plus ten percent of what the others earned as well. We watched kids at yard sales, baby-sat, weeded gardens, walked dogs, fed cats, helped people pack and clean, and did anything else we could come up with.

And the funny thing was, even though it was work, it was a lot of fun.

But business just about died after Labor Day. That weekend we'd done four yard sales, and we hadn't done one since then. There'd been some last-minute bulb planting in October, but that ended the gardening for the year. People came home from vacations, so there was no more need to feed cats, and lately it seemed as if even the dogs were walking themselves. That just about left baby-sitting, and the only one of us who worked at that regularly was my sister Carol.

Which reminded me. She'd worked the night before, and she hadn't given me the thirty cents she owed me. Thirty cents wasn't much, but it was the only income Kid Power would have for the week, and I wanted it.

"Carol!" I shouted, as I walked into the house.

"What?" Carol shouted back. Judging from the sound, she was in the living room. So I went there. Sure enough, she was sitting in front of the TV, watching a football game with my father.

"You owe me thirty cents," I told her, as I plopped down on the sofa next to her.

"I do not," she said. "Why should I owe you anything?"

"You worked last night, didn't you?" I said. "You baby-sat for three hours at a dollar an hour, and I'm entitled to ten percent of that. Thirty cents."

"Forget it," Carol said. "I'm not paying you any thirty cents."

"But you owe me," I shrieked.

"I paid you when the jobs came in from Kid Power," Carol replied. "But I got this job on my own, so why should I pay you anything?"

"You got the job because you were recommended by

somebody you got through Kid Power," I told her. "That's the same thing as getting the job through Kid Power. Isn't it, Dad?"

"Third down," Dad said. "Wait until this play is over, and then ask me."

So we sat quietly while the quarterback tried to pass the ball. It was incomplete, so Dad turned to us. "Now what seems to be the problem?" he asked.

"Carol owes me thirty cents, and she won't pay," I told him.

"Janie has this fantasy that Kid Power is still in business," Carol said. "And she expects me to keep shelling out ten percent of my hard-earned money for no reason whatsoever."

"Kid Power is too in business," I said.

"Yeah?" Carol said. "Name the last job you worked on."

Unfortunately, that took a lot of thought. If things had gone the way I wanted, I would have been checking in every day on my friend Mrs. Edwards, and that would have counted, since she paid me fifty cents a visit. But Mrs. Edwards broke her hip over the summer, and ever since she got home, she'd had a nurse's aide coming in to help her, so she didn't need me anymore. "I raked leaves," I replied.

"When?" Carol asked.

"A couple of weeks ago," I admitted. Once you'd raked all the leaves, there wasn't that much left to do. "But that doesn't mean Kid Power is dead."

"Nobody said it was dead," Dad said. "But you haven't been doing much with it lately. Which is fine with me. Your schoolwork is a lot more important than making a little extra money. Especially now that you have your bike."

"But Carol is still working," I said. "She has her paper route, and her baby-sitting, and you don't mind that."

"I have to have those jobs," Carol said. "I'm saving for something really important."

"What?" I asked. The original plan had been that Carol would use her money for a new bike, too, but she'd bought that in August.

"I'm saving to go to Paris," she declared.

"What?" I asked. Even Dad looked surprised.

"Not this summer," she said. "I won't have enough money this summer. But with the money I earn for the next two years, I'll have enough to go on a chaperoned high school trip for a month in France. I am taking French, after all. The trip will be very educational."

"That's very impressive, Carol," Dad said, just the way she wanted him to. I just shuddered. If Carol was planning to save up for two whole years for something educational, I'd never see another penny out of her again. Carol had always been a tightwad, but now she'd have Dad on her side every time she refused to give me the money she owed me. Kid Power was a definite goner.

"I read about the trip in a magazine," Carol said. "And I didn't want to mention it to you and Mom until I was sure I could save up the money on my own. I didn't want to be an added burden to you. Especially with Mom just starting her own business."

Not only was Kid Power a goner; after that speech, I probably was, too. Dad and Mom would decide they could only afford one kid, and Carol was bound to be first choice. I wondered if my grandmother would be willing to take me in for the next six years.

"I'm proud of you, Carol," Dad said. "You know what you want, and you're willing to go after it without looking to other people for help."

I had spent the entire summer working, and Dad never once made a speech like that to me. It was always "I don't approve" or "You shouldn't be doing that" or "Why don't you quit already?" Carol only had to say she planned to spend hundreds and hundreds of dollars, and Dad was ready to give her the Nobel Prize for Economics.

"What's Carol up to?" Mom asked, walking into the living room. I liked the way she put that, so I smiled up at her.

"I'm saving up money for a chaperoned high school summer tour of France," Carol declared. "I'm hoping to go the summer after next."

"That sounds great," Mom said, perching on the arm of Dad's chair. " I'm sure your father and I will be happy to help."

"Thanks, Mom," Carol said. "Let me see how much I can earn on my own first, though. I know money is still a little tight around here."

"We have more than enough for our needs," Dad said.

"Besides," Mom said, "Something Extra is going great. By a year from next summer, I should be a multi-millionaire."

I sighed to myself. Mom had come up with the idea of Something Extra from watching me at work with Kid Power. She had decided there were a lot of odd jobs adults could do, and a lot of housewives who would like a little extra income. So she sent out fliers, and hired about ten women who could make gourmet meals, and house-sit for people who were expecting the plumber but couldn't take the day off from work, and do housecleaning, and help shut-ins, and organize birthday parties for kids, and buy groceries, and do all kinds of jobs. The camera she'd just bought was to take pictures at parties, so that the parents wouldn't have to. She hadn't made her fortune yet, but things were looking promising. And even though she always gave me credit for the idea, she refused to give me ten percent of her ten percent.

I stared at my family then, and had one of those moments where everything is completely clear. Everyone in my family had a goal. My father loved his work as a labor lawyer, and he believed in what he was doing. Mom was hard at work starting her own business; I'd never seen her so excited about anything. Even Carol was working toward something, a trip a year and a half away. And all I had were my memories of Kid Power. I was twelve years old, and already I was living in the past.

"That reminds me," Carol said. "Would you mind taking down that stupid sign of yours?"

"Which sign?" I asked. I was too depressed to complain about her calling it stupid.

"The one in the supermarket," Carol said.

"But you made that sign," I said. Carol had made all my signs; her lettering was a lot better than mine.

"It was stupid when I made it," Carol said. "Actually it was very nice-looking then. But nobody's calling you anymore, and people have scribbled all over it. You really should take it down."

"Sure," I said, all the fight knocked out of me. "I'll take it down."

"Good," Dad said. "Kid Power was fine as a summer project, but I'm just as happy it's finished."

Right then I felt as if I was finished. No signs, no jobs, no ten percent. Just a bike and a few memories.

I walked over to the window and stared out at the street.

It was the week before Thanksgiving, and already everything was gray. There were still leaves on the ground, but the trees were all bare. The days were so short they were over before they began. It was definitely winter, and Kid Power was a thing of the past. Soon it would be snowing.

"Snow," I said.

"What?" Mom asked. Dad and Carol were engrossed in the football game again.

"It's going to be snowing soon," I said.

"Not too soon, I hope," she replied. "I haven't put the snow tires on the car yet."

"How about if I shovel the snow for you?" I asked.

"Are you volunteering?" Mom asked.

"For pay," I said. "How about if we agree right now that I'll shovel the walk automatically. You won't have to holler at me, or try to convince Carol to do it. I'll do it every snowstorm for pay."

"How much?" Mom asked.

I thought about it. Kid Power had charged a dollar an hour, but I didn't think snow shoveling should be paid for on that basis. "A dollar fifty per sidewalk," I said. "Two dollars for driveways."

"And you absolutely promise you'll do it automatically and not complain or run off to build a snowman or say you want to sleep late?" Mom asked.

"I absolutely promise," I said.

"You're on," Mom said. "It'll be worth it not to worry about who's going to get it done."

"Do you think other people would feel that way?" I asked her.

"Probably," Mom said. "Snow is such a nuisance."

"It is, isn't it," I said, suddenly happy again. "I'll bet I could get lots of people to hire me."

"Maybe," Mom said. "But there's only so much you can do. For one thing, you can only travel so far. I'm not going to drive you all over town just so you can shovel people's walks."

I hadn't thought of that. For a moment I was stumped.

And then I remembered how Kid Power Agency worked. I helped other kids get jobs, and they gave me ten percent of what they earned. There was no reason why we couldn't do the same thing with snow shoveling. My friends all lived in different parts of town. All I'd have to do was get them the jobs shoveling the walks in their neighborhoods, and I'd end up rich.

"I'll get my friends," I told Mom. "It'll be just like last summer."

"But last summer you were saving for something," Mom pointed out. "You got your bike today. What do you want to earn money for?"

"A computer!" I shouted. "To keep track of the business."

"What business?" Carol asked, looking up from the TV set.

"Kid Power," I said. "Come on, Carol. I need a new sign."

"Oh, no," Dad groaned. "Not this again."

I didn't pay any attention to him. Kid Power was back in business, and so was I.

Chapter 2

The first thing I had to prove to myself and everybody else was that there really was a market for Kid Power's new winter service.

"Don't overbook," my mother warned me as I set out the next morning to convince my neighbors to hire me. "You can only do so much."

"I won't," I promised. My fantasy of course had been that every house on the block would hire me, but even I knew that was crazy. I only had two arms, after all, and one back. So I figured if I could get just three other households I should be satisfied. That would be six dollars for sidewalks (including my family's), and eight dollars if they took me on for driveways, too. Fourteen dollars a snowstorm could be a big help in my savings for a computer.

It was funny. I hadn't even known I wanted a computer until I said I did. But now I wanted one a lot. No successful business could be run without one, I pointed out to my mother, who didn't have one for Something Extra yet.

I decided to start my sales pitch with Mrs. Edwards, since I was pretty sure she'd agree. So I knocked on her door, and I was happy when she opened it herself. That meant she was feeling better. She was still using a walker, though.

"Kid Power is back in business," I told her. "We've decided to go into snow removal."

"What a good idea," Mrs. Edwards said. "Have you found many customers?"

"I came to you first," I admitted. "We'll be charging a dollar fifty for sidewalks and two dollars for driveways. The important thing is that if you agree to our terms now, you'll never have to worry again about who's going to shovel for you."

"I don't use my driveway anymore," Mrs. Edwards said. "My nurse's aide parks on the street, and I don't drive anymore. But it would be a great convenience if you shoveled my walk. Can I hire you for sidewalks only?"

Of course I would have preferred it if she'd agreed to the package deal, but I could see her point. Why pay for something you don't need? "You're on," I said. "I'll shovel every single snowfall of four inches or more."

"How about if you just shovel automatically, even if there's less than four inches?" Mrs. Edwards suggested. "I'll pay you the same rate, of course."

"All right," I said. "If there isn't enough snow to shovel, I'll sweep it off the sidewalk for you."

"Thank you very much," Mrs. Edwards said. "And I'll be sure to recommend Kid Power to my friends. You did save my life, after all."

I blushed. Rescuing people wasn't one of Kid Power's regular services. "I'd better get going," I said. "I want to talk to other people on the block, too."

"Good luck, Janie," Mrs. Edwards said, but I was sure I wouldn't need it. I was offering a needed service. According to my mother, that was what made a business a success.

I started walking from door to door. A lot of people weren't home. I tried to remember who wasn't in, so I could go back and try them again. Finally I got an answer to my ring.

"My name is Janie Golden, and I represent Kid Power," I said, trying to sound grown up. "I'd like to offer you our special snow-removal services."

"I gave at the office," the man said, and slammed the door in my face.

I considered quitting on the spot. But that wasn't how fortunes were made. So I walked over to the next house and rang the bell. A woman opened the door. She had two little kids grabbing at her legs.

"My name is Janie Golden," I said. "I represent Kid Power. I'd like to offer you our special snow-removal services."

"It isn't snowing yet, is it?" the woman asked, trying to shake the kids off her. "Tell me it isn't snowing."

"Oh, it isn't, ma'am. Don't worry," I said. "But it will be before you know it. If you hire Kid Power now, you won't ever have to worry about who's going to shovel your walk."

"My husband always did that," the woman said. "I guess now I'll have to."

"Not if you hire Kid Power," I said. "We'll guarantee to shovel your sidewalk for a dollar fifty and your driveway for two dollars. That's for any snowfall of four inches or more. Are you interested?"

"Stop biting my leg, Seth," the woman said to one of the kids. "David, stop biting Seth's leg. Sure. Why not? I guess it will be one less thing to worry about."

"Great," I said. "You'll see me at the first snowfall."

"Which I hope won't be for at least eight months," the woman said. "I haven't put the snow tires on my car yet."

I wished I could put snow tires on for people; there was obviously a lot of money to be made doing that. But one thing I'd learned the summer before was never to take on jobs I couldn't handle. So I just smiled at the lady and at Seth and David and went to the next house, to see if they'd be interested.

They weren't, and neither were people in the next seven houses I asked at. It wasn't very encouraging, and I considered stopping at two and a half jobs. But then I thought about the computer, and how if I got one before Mom did, I could rent her time on it for Something Extra. So I kept knocking on doors.

After a half-hour, I found another person willing to listen. I told her my terms, and she stared at me thoughtfully.

"Here's my problem," the woman said. "My husband had a heart attack a couple of years ago. Not a big one, just one of those little warning shots. So Herm gave up smoking, and he lost twenty pounds, and now he exercises, and he's really in fine health."

"That's great," I said.

"But he still thinks he can do all those things he used to do," the woman continued. "Like shoveling snow. That's the quickest way to a heart attack, you know."

I didn't know. I began worrying about my own heart as soon as she told me.

"If the walk gets shoveled before Herm has a chance to do it, then he won't be able to complain," the woman continued. "But if you were just the least bit late, then Herm would probably go out and start shoveling by himself, and you know what would happen then."

I nodded. Herm would have a heart attack, and it would be all my fault.

Of course, if I decided not to take on Herm and his sidewalk, he would have the heart attack anyway, and it would still be all my fault. The only solution was for me to take the job and keep Herm from ever looking at a shovel again.

"I'll do you first," I promised. "That way Herm won't have a chance."

The woman smiled at me, which made me feel better. I probably shouldn't have called her husband Herm, but I felt as if I knew him. His life was in my hands, after all. "Sidewalks and driveways," she said. "First thing after the snow stops."

"You're on," I said, and we shook hands on it. I wondered if Herm would ever know how I was keeping him alive. Maybe he would think elves shoveled the walk for him. But I figured that was between him and his wife. My job was to shovel.

So I walked home, adding the numbers up in my head. Three driveways at two dollars each, and four sidewalks at a dollar fifty. That came to twelve dollars per snowfall. Assuming there were four snowfalls that winter, that was forty-eight dollars right there, and all it would cost me was a sore back. We already owned a shovel, after all.

The next thing I had to do was get jobs for all my friends, so they'd have to pay me ten percent. Of course, first I'd have to get them to agree to the whole idea.

I made my first phone call to my best friend Lisa. Lisa and I had had a big fight over Kid Power last summer, but then I'd hired her, and we got to be friends again. Lisa's specialty was gardening, but she wasn't afraid of hard work. Or so I told myself while I dialed her number.

"I liked earning money last summer," Lisa admitted, when I finished telling her the plan. "But I don't know about shoveling snow."

"It's easy money," I said. "All you have to do is work in the morning, and then you have the rest of the day to do whatever you want in."

"Sometimes it snows all day," Lisa said. "And then you'd have to shovel in the evening, when it's dark and cold."

"Maybe in the afternoon," I said. "But never at night. And the money is really good."

Lisa sighed. "Are you going to go crazy over this?" she asked. "Like you did last summer?"

"Never," I said. "Really. This isn't like last summer. It's just whenever it snows. It doesn't snow that much here. Maybe twice a winter."

"Maybe six times," Lisa said. My heart leaped when I thought about how much more money I could earn if it snowed six times.

"Besides, it's a public service," I told her. Lisa has a very soft heart. "We'll be keeping people from having heart attacks. Shoveling snow is the first step to a heart attack, you know."

"I don't know," Lisa said, but I could tell she was weakening.

"I'm going to be working for four people," I said. "But that doesn't mean you have to do that many. You could just take on two walks, for example. And then, if you liked it, maybe we could get you more work later in the winter."

"You are going crazy," Lisa said with a sigh. "I can tell, Janie."

"Then go crazy with me," I said. "Come on, Lisa. It'll be fun."

Lisa sighed even harder. "Maybe you won't be able to get anybody to hire me," she said.

"Then I can try?" I asked.

"All right," she said. "But I only want two other people, plus my parents."

"You won't regret it," I said.

"I already regret it," Lisa replied. "How many other kids are you going to exploit?"

"As many as I can," I told her. "I figured I'd call Ted next."

"Good choice," she said. "Ted actually likes to do stuff like this. Let me know how it goes."

"I sure will," I said. "Thanks, Lisa."

"You're welcome," she said, with the biggest sigh of all. Lisa had very impressive sighs. I hung up, called Ted, and told him my plan.

"You'll get the people to hire me?" he asked.

"That's the idea," I said.

"Including my parents?" he continued.

"Don't you think you could convince them better than I could?" I asked.

"They expect me to do that stuff for free," he said.

"Well, if they see that other people are willing to pay you for your work, maybe they'll agree to pay you, too," I said. "That is the American way, after all."

"Get me four jobs," Ted said. "And then we'll tackle my parents."

· I didn't really look forward to tackling Ted's parents, but nobody ever said making a fortune would be easy. So I agreed, hung up, and tried my friend Margie.

"I love snow," Margie said. "I love shoveling."

"You do?" I asked. Margie always surprised me.

"It's practically my favorite thing to do," Margie replied. "After taking care of kids, that is. I don't suppose I could take care of kids while I shovel the walks?"

I thought about Seth and David, but I couldn't figure out a way for Margie to shovel and baby-sit simultaneously. Still, it was worth thinking about, once I had Kid Power's winter program in full swing.

"So you'll let me get you some snow-shoveling jobs?" I asked.

"Four of them," Margie replied. "Thank you, Janie."

Margie was definitely the sort of person Kid Power needed more of. I told her so, and she thanked me again.

That left only Sheila from the kids Kid Power had used last summer. Sheila was a problem, though. Her mother changed her phone number a lot, so it wasn't always possible to get through to her. Besides, Sheila didn't strike me as the snow-shoveling type. Not that Margie had, either, but Margie I knew I could trust. I decided against asking Sheila to join us. Maybe later in the winter, when Kid Power had expanded, but not until then.

The next step was to get everybody the customers I'd just promised them. I ran downstairs and made myself a sandwich. Then I grabbed my bike and rode over to Lisa's neighborhood first, to knock on doors.

Lisa lived in a fancy section of town, and all the houses had long stretches of sidewalk and driveway. I didn't blame her for not wanting to shovel everybody's, but on the other hand, it seemed like a good selling point.

I heard the background sounds of football games on in most of the houses, and I mostly spoke to women. It wasn't easy selling the service, but I'd gotten used to rejection that morning. Besides, one sale made me feel so good that it took care of ten rejections. And since I was only trying for two sales, the pressure wasn't too bad.

I got the first one fairly easily, but the second one was taking forever. I checked out the other houses in the neighborhood, trying to find an especially friendly looking one.

What I saw instead was the biggest house in town. Lisa lived two blocks away from Mrs. Dell, the richest person in our county. Years ago, there had been a Mr. Dell, and he had been rich, too, so when he married Mrs. Dell, they got even richer together. Now Mrs. Dell was a widow living all alone, except for her housekeeper, in a genuine mansion.

But her mansion didn't interest me nearly as much as her sidewalk and driveway did. They were both endless. The driveway was the circular kind that winds around and around. And the sidewalk was at least twice the length of anybody else's.

It wouldn't be fair to ask Lisa to shovel Mrs. Dell's

walk all by herself. Then again, we'd have to charge more than the three-fifty combined price. Five dollars at least, and seven if we could get it. I decided to ask for seven and bargain down if I had to.

It took all my nerve to walk up to the door and ring the bell. I reminded myself that Mrs. Dell was about the same age as Mrs. Edwards, and I had no trouble talking with her. She'd been my easiest sale, and she had a lot less sidewalk to clear than Mrs. Dell did.

Mrs. Dell opened the door herself, so I figured the housekeeper must have the day off. It was Sunday, after all.

I smiled my biggest smile at Mrs. Dell and told her my name. "I represent Kid Power," I said. "We're offering a special prewinter snow-shoveling plan."

"That's lovely," Mrs. Dell said. "My brother used to do that when he was a boy. And now girls are doing it, too. How very sensible."

"Thank you," I said. "Does that mean you're interested in our plan?"

"Absolutely," Mrs. Dell said. "Industry should always be rewarded in the young. Twenty-five."

"Twenty-five dollars?" I gasped. It was a big walk, but I hadn't realized it was that big. Of course, Mrs. Dell was rich, and she did want to reward industry.

"Oh, no, of course not," Mrs. Dell said, and she laughed. "Twenty-five cents. My brother only charged a dime, but times have changed."

"I'm sorry," I said, although it nearly broke my heart. "We can't do it at that price."

"Oh, well," Mrs. Dell said. "Let me know if you change your mind."

"I will," I said, knowing I never would. There were plenty of houses left for me to try that afternoon, and after school for a while if I had to. I was determined to get good-paying jobs for everyone in Kid Power before the first flake of snow fell.

Chapter 3

"I don't believe this," Mom said, staring out the window on the Sunday after Thanksgiving. "Look at it come down."

So I looked. I didn't believe it either, but what was upsetting my mother was making me very happy. The snow was falling hard and heavy, and what had looked like autumn the day before was now definitely winter.

"I still don't have the snow tires on!" Mom wailed. "And now I won't be able to drive to the garage to have them put on because of the snow."

I tried to feel sorry for her, but I couldn't. All that snow meant I was about to earn Kid Power's first real money in months. I'd found work for all my friends, too, so I'd be collecting a lot of ten percents as well. Kid Power's computer was just a few dozen blizzards away. And if it was going to start snowing in November, who knew when it would stop? We'd had a heavy snowfall the year before in the middle of April; that could happen again. If it snowed twice a month between now and then, we'd all end up very rich.

"Do you think it's letting up now?" I asked Mom. It

had been snowing since early that morning, and I'd promised Lisa that it would never stop right before dark, so that she would have to shovel at night.

"I guess so," Mom said glumly. "I knew I should have had the snow tires put on last week."

"I think I'm going to go out and start shoveling people's walks," I said, thinking of Herm. "Don't worry, I'll be doing ours, but we're going to be last."

"That's the least of my worries," Mom said. "Bundle up, Janie, and don't overdo."

"I will," I said. "And I won't." I guess Mom understood me, since she didn't say anything back. She just kept staring out the window and sighing.

I got the shovel and went to work. By the time I finished Herm's driveway, I would have been happy to quit. I'd forgotten what backbreaking work shoveling was. I kept reminding myself that I was the only thing standing between Herm and a heart attack, but that was very little comfort as I sweated and shivered.

Getting paid by Herm's wife Gert helped, though. Feeling those dollar bills in my pocket eased the ache of my muscles and gave me the strength I needed to go over to my second customer's house and dig there. I realized I had never learned Seth and David's mom name, so while I cleared off her sidewalk and drive, I made up names for her. I'd finally decided on Coradora Appalora when I finished her driveway. I never wanted to see another driveway again. I no longer even knew why people drove, especially since they never put the snow tires on their cars.

When Coradora paid me, I asked her what her name was. It turned out not to be Coradora at all, just Gail Howard.

I didn't tell her the name I'd come up with. You never know what's going to offend people.

My next stop was Mrs. Edward's house, and I was really grateful I didn't have to shovel her driveway. I kept remembering Mrs. Dell's circular drive and how she'd offered to pay a quarter to get it done. At that point, I wouldn't have done it for a million dollars, not that she was likely to offer it to me.

Shoveling Mrs. Edwards's sidewalk felt like nothing after the work I'd done, and she gave me home-baked cookies when I was finished. That gave me all the strength I needed to return home and shovel there. I have to admit I didn't do as good a job at home as I had at Herm's, or even Gail's, but I did well enough so that we could get out if we wanted to. I cleared off the shovel, put it back in the garage, and came back in. I sat on the radiator for a few minutes, until I defrosted, and then I got paid by Mom. Then I went upstairs and counted the twelve dollars over and over again.

When I had absolutely convinced myself that twelve dollars was twelve dollars, I started calling the other kids to see how they were doing. Lisa was already home, but Margie and Ted were still shoveling. So I rested on my bed and thought about all the ten percents they owed me. Out of a sense of great generosity, I decided not to take ten percent of the money they earned from their parents. But even without that, they still owed me three fifty. Never being able to move again was a small price to pay for fifteen fifty. I fell asleep fully dressed on my bed, trying to decide what sort of computer to buy.

The next day at school, Ted and Lisa and Margie paid what they owed me. I put the money in an envelope, so I wouldn't get it mixed up with my lunch money.

"What are you doing there, Golden?"

I looked up at the sound of the voice and saw Johnny Richards. Johnny was in Carol's grade, and I knew him mostly through her. He was a real creep, big and mean. I shoved my money into the envelope and pushed the envelope into my pants pocket. If Johnny wanted it, he was going to have to steal it from me.

"What do you want?" I asked him, trying to keep my voice from quaking.

"I don't want anything," he said. "I was just wondering what you were doing, taking money from this kid here, and stuffing it in your pocket like that. That's all. A perfectly innocent question."

There was nothing innocent about Johnny, and we both knew it. I considered refusing to answer his question, but then I decided that would be a mistake. "This is my friend," I said. "And she owed me some money for Kid Power. That's all."

"Kid Power," Johnny said. "Oh, yeah, I know that. I saw the sign up in the supermarket. You do jobs."

"Right," I said. "We're shoveling snow this winter, that's all."

"I shovel snow, too," Johnny said. "All my friends, we shovel snow. Are you gonna take our business away from us?"

"Of course not," I said, trying to smile at him. "We just have a few contracts with people. You probably have lots and lots of people's walks to clear. We just have a few."

"A few too many," Johnny said. "Listen here, Golden, I don't like the idea of anybody muscling in on my territory. See what I mean?"

"Don't worry," I said. No reason for him to; I was

* 27 *

worrying enough for both of us. "It's a big town. There's lots of snow. We'll both end up rich by the time winter's over."

"How much are you charging?" Johnny asked. I noticed Margie slipping away from us. I certainly didn't blame her.

"A dollar fifty for sidewalks, two dollars for driveways," I said. Maybe all he wanted was some business tips. I'd certainly be happy to supply him with those if he spared my life.

"That's less than I charge," Johnny replied. "A lot less. You trying to undercut me?"

"Oh, no," I said. "We just charge less because we don't do nearly as good a job as you probably do. I'm sure you do quality work. You're so strong and everything." I swallowed hard. It might not have been a good idea to remind Johnny just how strong he was.

"Me and my friends plan to stay in business," Johnny informed me. His smile made my intestines shrivel. "We'll do what we have to, to see to that, Golden. Get my meaning?"

"I can certainly respect that," I said. "No problem, Johnny. You shovel your jobs, and we'll shovel ours."

"I don't know about that," he said. "You'd better be careful, Golden, or you're going to end up on the wrong end of the shovel."

"I'll be careful," I said. "Thanks for the warning, Johnny. Oops, I'd better be running. I had no idea how late it was. Bye." And I scurried down the hallway into the safety of the cafeteria.

I sat down at the table next to Lisa and Margie. "Margie told me what was happening," Lisa said. "Do you think Johnny is going to cause trouble?"

"Of course not," I said. "There's plenty of work for all of us. Besides, it may never snow again. Maybe all we'll have from now on is rain because of the greenhouse effect. You know about that. The world is warming up, and places where it used to snow are turning into Florida. No more snow here, I'll bet. One snowfall at Thanksgiving time, and then it's surf's up for the rest of the winter."

"I don't think we should count on the greenhouse effect," Margie said.

"I'll talk to my father," I replied. "Sometimes he has very good advice on problems."

"Maybe," Lisa said. I could see she was thinking about quitting altogether. I knew it wouldn't take much to get everybody to quit. We were all suffering from aching muscles. And the other kids might not have an important goal, as I did. A talk with my father was definitely in order.

I waited until after supper to bring up the subject with him. Dad had gone into the den to read, so I followed him upstairs and knocked on the door.

"What can I do for you?" he asked me, as I sat down.

"There's this guy," I said. "Johnny Richards. Carol's mentioned him because he's in her grade. He's a big bully."

"Sounds familiar," Dad said. "Is Carol having problems with him?"

"I am," I said, and I told Dad about the conversation Johnny and I had had. Dad nodded thoughtfully when I finished.

"That's what happens in the open marketplace," he said. "You didn't think you were going to have a monopoly, did you?"

"What's a monopoly?" I asked. I knew what the game was, but I had the feeling Dad was talking about something else.

"It's when you're the only person doing a certain kind of business," Dad explained. "Suppose there were only one kind of car manufacturer. Then it would have a monopoly on the car industry."

"That sounds good," I said. "I like that."

"Sure you do," Dad said, "you little capitalist exploiter of the masses. If you have a monopoly on something, you can control what it's going to cost. Since there's no competition, people can't buy your product anywhere else, so they have to pay what you ask."

"It's sounding better and better," I said. "How do you get to be a monopoly?"

"You buy your own country and make up your own rules," Dad said. "In the United States, we try to avoid monopolies for the most part. We're big on freedom of choice around here."

"But if I had a monopoly, Johnny would have to leave me alone," I said.

"And if Johnny had one, you'd have to leave him alone," Dad replied.

"That isn't fair," I said. "It was my idea to get Kid Power into snow shoveling. I thought of it first."

"I doubt that Johnny sees it that way," Dad said. "It sounds as if he was shoveling snow last winter, before there even was a Kid Power."

"Does that mean I have to give it up?" I asked. "Just because he got there first? He was born before me, so he had a head start."

"Neither one of you has to give up anything," Dad said. "First of all, there are plenty of walks to shovel.

But even if there weren't, that's what the open market-place is all about. Whoever does the better job will get more customers. It doesn't sound as if Johnny is going to keep his because of his charming personality and delightful smile."

"I don't want his customers," I said, thinking about my aching back. "I just don't want him to steal mine."

"Well, you're going to have to be careful, then," Dad said. "Because if he wants to, he can get into a price war with you."

"What's a price war?" I asked. It sounded like a place where people threw prices at each other.

"It's a way of taking business away from your competition," Dad replied. "Suppose Johnny decides to offer prices lower than yours. Your customers might all go over to him. And then you might decide to cut your prices, too, and maybe go after his customers. You could each slash your prices until you're barely making a profit. Price wars are good for customers, but bad for businesses."

My head was starting to ache almost as much as my back. "You don't think that's going to happen, do you?" I asked. I wasn't sure I could bear it if it did.

"No," Dad said. "I doubt that Johnny has the imagination to think of lowering his prices. And since yours are already lower than his, there's no reason for you to cut yours."

"What else could he do to me?" I asked.

"Not much," Dad said. "After all, if he does something really wrong, we'll contact his parents. Even the police, if necessary. And I'm sure he knows that. Most likely, he'll just growl at you and try to intimidate you. If you stand your ground, you should be fine."

"Then that's what I'll do," I said. "I'll stand my ground and make sure Kid Power does the best possible job and hope that Johnny keeps all of his old customers, and then we'll all be happy."

"Excellent," Dad said. "I'm glad you respect Johnny's needs, too. Sometimes I think you want Kid Power to take over the entire world."

"Me?" I said, trying to look innocent. "You really think I want that?"

Dad raised his eyebrows at me. "That's exactly what I think," he said. "Are you going to try to deny it?"

"See you later, Dad," I said instead, and left the den fast. I didn't really want Kid Power to take over the entire world. At least not before I had my computer set up so I'd know what to do with the world once I got it.

I don't know whether it was the new sign Carol made for me that I put up in the supermarket, or the sight of so much snow left on sidewalks and driveways all over town, but that week Kid Power got a dozen calls from people wanting to make arrangements for snow removal that winter. Most of the calls came from people who had used Kid Power the summer before, and it felt nice hearing from them and knowing they were satisfied enough with Kid Power to hire us again.

Of course I had to find new kids to dig out all that snow, and that didn't prove too hard. Last summer a lot of kids had been away at camp or on trips, and I had a limited number of recruits. But everybody was around in December, so I just set up a meeting at my house for kids who were interested. Five kids showed up, and I divided the jobs among them. The computer was practically mine.

"You'll need it," Carol said, "to keep track of all those kids from all those jobs. One rotten apple, you know, and there goes Kid Power's reputation down the drain."

"There are no rotten apples," I told her. "Kid Power selects its workers very carefully."

Carol snorted. "Your workers are all friends of yours," she said. "What kind of selection is that?"

"The best," I said. "I wouldn't have a rotten apple for a friend. For a sister maybe, but not for a friend."

Lucky for me, the phone rang then. I ran to answer it, and it was another person wanting to use Kid Power that winter. I took down all the information, and promised the woman I'd get back to her. Kid Power was bigger than it had been even at its biggest last summer. Thank goodness for the open marketplace.

"I wish Something Extra would have a spurt of business like yours," Mom said at dinner that night.

"I thought things were going well," Dad said.

"They are," Mom said. "But it would be nice to quadruple our business in a week."

"Young businesses shouldn't expand too fast," Dad replied. "That can be almost as harmful as too slow growth."

"You don't think Kid Power is growing too fast, do you, Dad?" I asked.

"It depends on how much control you have over the kids who'll be working for you," Dad said. "Maybe it's time for you to hire some managers to help you out."

"But that would cost money," I said. I hated spending Kid Power's money.

"But if you can't run Kid Power properly without help, it'll just collapse," Dad replied.

"Then I'll just spend more time taking care of business," I declared.

"Not at the cost of your schoolwork, you won't,"

Dad said. "Kid Power is fine as long as it doesn't interfere with your studies. But school has to come first."

I sighed. As far as Dad was concerned, something always came before Kid Power.

"Hire me," Carol suggested. "That way the money will stay in the family."

"That's a wonderful idea," Mom said.

"Wait a second," I said. "You're asking me for a job, Carol?"

"I prefer to think of it as offering my little sister a helping hand," Carol replied. "You can assign some of the kids to me, and I'll make sure they do their work. For a small fee, of course."

"How small?" I asked. I had negotiated with Carol the summer before, and we usually ended up okay. But I still wasn't positive I trusted her.

"You get ten percent, right?" Carol asked, as though she didn't know. "That's thirty-five cents per job."

"Usually," I said. "Some people just want their walks shoveled." Actually, only Mrs. Edwards had asked for those terms, but I wasn't about to tell Carol that.

"I'll take twenty-five cents," she said. "That'll give you ten cents for doing absolutely nothing."

"I do something," I said. "I got all those jobs."

"They mostly came from the sign," Carol pointed out. "A sign that I made. It isn't as if you went from door to door to get the job. So why should you get all the extra money as a result of a sign that I made?"

"The sign may be all right," I said. "But the people never would have called if they didn't already know and respect Kid Power. And that had nothing to do with your stupid sign."

"Ah, good," Dad said. "This argument is finally deteriorating to a level I can understand."

"I don't see why I shouldn't be paid adequately if I'm going to be doing all the work," Carol said. She smiled smugly at me.

"I'm not going to give you twenty-five thirty-fifths of my profits," I told her.

"That's five sevenths," Carol said. "You're right; you do need a computer."

"Are you serious about a computer?" Dad asked.

"I'm saving up my money for one," I told him. "For Kid Power and Something Extra. But mostly for my schoolwork. It's an investment in the future."

"Sometimes I feel as if I'm living in the middle of a commercial," Dad said. "But a computer is a fine thing to save up for, Janie. If you don't mind saving for the next few years."

"That's why I don't want to spend too much money on managers," I said. "Every quarter Carol wants to take away from me is a quarter taken away from the computer. From my future success. Carol's selfishness might be keeping me from getting into an Ivy League college."

"I hardly think Carol's offer is selfish," Mom said. "Besides, you're only in the seventh grade. You still have plenty of time to make it to the Ivy League with or without a computer."

"Fifteen cents a job," I said. "That's fifteen for Carol and twenty for me."

"Never," Carol said.

"I don't have to hire you," I said. "I don't have to hire anybody. But even if I do hire somebody, it sure doesn't have to be you."

"But just think how nice it would be to keep Kid Power in the family," Mom said. "And convenient, too."

"I'll take twenty cents," Carol said, "even though that's hardly enough to pay for my time."

"What time?" I shrieked. "All you'll have to do is make a couple of phone calls on days that it snows. You're on the phone all the time anyway."

"All right," Carol said. "But if I don't take the job, then you'll have to be on the phone yourself making those calls. And you've told me how important it is for you to get right over to those people's houses and start shoveling. Even if you get somebody else to manage, you'll have to call her to make sure she's doing her job. With me, you can see me make the calls before you go out shoveling. I'm worth the price I'm asking."

"Now I know I'm in the middle of a commercial," Dad said.

"We split it fifty-fifty," I said. "You get seventeen and a half cents, and I get seventeen and a half cents. Only if it comes to an odd number, I get the extra halfpenny. Deal?"

Carol thought about it. Dad and Mom held their breath. "All right," she said. "And I'll be in charge of all the new kids, how's that? All the jobs that have come in this week."

"Okay," I said, secretly relieved. I hadn't really wanted to check up on each and every one of those kids on my own. Having Carol do it for me would be a big help. Besides, I liked the idea of having her work for me again. "Just remember, I can fire you."

"Just remember, I can destroy you," Carol replied, and we shook hands on it. I had the very strong feeling that Carol had gotten exactly what she wanted, but she usually did. There are some real disadvantages to negotiating with a big sister.

"Peace," Dad said. "It's wonderful."

So then the phone rang. We all sighed, and I got up to answer it.

"Is this Kid Power?" a woman asked.

"It sure is," I said.

"My name is Mrs. Lucini," the woman said. "I live on Oak Street."

"Sure," I said, scribbling the information down. Between Mom's business and mine, we always made sure to have a pad and pencil by every phone in the house.

"I'm not as young as I used to be," Mrs. Lucini said. "Actually I'm seventy-nine years old."

"Wow," I said respectfully.

"I saw your sign up at the supermarket, and I remembered reading about you last summer when you saved that woman's life," Mrs. Lucini continued.

I smiled at the memory. The local paper had run a big article about me and Kid Power when that happened, and I got a lot of business out of it.

"So it occurred to me that maybe you could help," Mrs. Lucini said. "I live alone, and my daughter-in-law comes over whenever she can, but I can't always count on her, because of her children. So I thought maybe I could hire Kid Power to come over every afternoon after school to run errands with me."

"Oh, sure," I said. "Running errands is one of Kid Power's specialities."

"Wonderful," Mrs. Lucini said. "I don't get around as well as I used to, but I hate the idea of being a shut-in all winter long. This way, one of you can help me walk on icy sidewalks and cross streets and carry my packages."

"Oh, I see," I said. "You want a walking companion."

"That's it exactly," Mrs. Lucini replied. "For maybe an hour a day. Some days, of course, I won't need to go out, so you should call first."

"Kid Power charges a dollar an hour," I told her.

"It would be well worth it," she said, "to know I'll have somebody with me to protect me from all the icy patches. Can I count on you to supply a companion?"

"Absolutely," I said. "It will be our pleasure."

"Fine," Mrs. Lucini said. She gave me her address and phone number, and I promised her I would send a kid over the next day for her approval.

"Carol!" I shouted, as I got off the phone. "I need your help."

"It'll cost you," Carol replied.

"Ah," Dad said. "Sisterly love."

"Kid Power is expanding," I said, telling her about my conversation with Mrs. Lucini.

"This could be big," Carol said. "Regular work for anyone who wants it. All we have to do is let all the old people know about Kid Power's newest service."

"Don't call them old people," Mom said. "Senior citizens. Village elders, maybe."

"Let's give Mrs. Lucini to Lisa," I said. "She doesn't really want to shovel snow anyway, and she's great with older people."

"Fine," Carol said. "We'll make up a chart and see who we can give her snow-shoveling jobs to. And, of course, we'll split the commissions on all senior citizen work as well."

"Okay," I said. "But you have to help us get jobs."

"I'll make up a new sign tonight," Carol said. "We'll put it up at the senior citizen center."

"Big bucks," I said. "We're going to end up so rich, Carol."

"Paris, here I come!" she sang.

"You know, I wouldn't mind taking one of the companion jobs myself," I said. "It wouldn't be all that different than what I did last summer for Mrs. Edwards. And I could use the steady money. Five dollars a week, even if it never snows again."

"Fine," Carol said. "It's too much for me to take on, but you have the time. And old people like you. I mean senior citizens. They think you're cute."

"I am cute," I said. "Aren't I, Mom?"

But Mom wasn't listening. "How do you do it?" she asked. "Kid Power just keeps expanding. All you do is put up a sign in the supermarket and the calls just pour in."

"Now, don't worry, Meg," Dad said. "Something Extra will grow in its own good time."

"And if it doesn't, we'll hire you, Mom," Carol said. "I'm sure Janie can find something for you in upper management."

"Sure, Mom," I said, sincerely hoping that would never happen. It would be tough enough firing Carol if I had to. I had the feeling there were laws forbidding you to fire your mother.

"See, Meg?" Dad said. "I always knew our children would provide for us in our old age. Just be prepared to negotiate."

"Advertising," Mom said. "We've been underadvertising. I think I'll see how much some radio ads would cost us. People need to hear about Something Extra."

"Free publicity is the best publicity," I told her. "Mrs. Lucini remembered me from the article in the paper last summer. You need to have an article about you."

"You're right," Mom said, thumping her fingers on the table. "I need a publicity stunt."

"Nothing with elephants, please," Dad said. "I can't stand publicity stunts with elephants."

"Do something for somebody famous," I suggested. "Then when the paper writes about him, they'll write about you, too."

"You're right," Mom said. "If Something Extra handled an important birthday party, that would make the paper."

I'd actually been thinking more along the lines of Something Extra saving somebody's life. But that sort of thing didn't happen every day of the week. Birthdays sure did.

"I have it," Dad said. "And it doesn't involve any elephants. Arrange a birthday party for Elvira Butsworth."

"Elvira Butsworth is dead, Dad," Carol said.

"I guess that would make it a surprise party," I said.

"Listen to me," Dad said. "Elvira Butsworth founded this town, right? And her statue stands in front of City Hall. All the kids have to learn about her, and all the parents have to listen to what their kids learn. Everybody in this town knows who Elvira Butsworth was."

"But nobody knows when her birthday is," Mom pointed out. "I suppose I could look it up, but what if it's in July? I need something now."

"So make it a party in honor of Elvira Butsworth," Dad said. "The idea is to do something big and splashy that's bound to be in the paper. If you can pull off a party for a town founder who's been dead for a hundred and fifty years, you'll be certain to get great publicity."

"It could be fun, Mom," Carol said. "And if you could get the schools involved, just think of all the extra publicity that would give you."

"There are never enough parties in January," I said. "I'll bet everybody would go to an Elvira Butsworth Day party if you threw one."

"It's certainly worth thinking about," Mom agreed. "Now, who's going to do the dishes while I think?"

"I will," Dad said, "if Janie and Carol promise to go upstairs and get to work on their homework immediately."

So we agreed. When we were all multimillionaires we'd get a dishwasher, I decided. Or only eat off paper plates. And the way things were going, that should be only a year or so away.

Chapter

5

I was having a wonderful dream about Kid Power making so much money that I bought not only a computer but the entire country of France, when I heard a knock at my bedroom door. It took me a moment to wake up enough to say, "Come in."

My mother stuck her head in. "It's Margie," she said. "She's on the phone for you."

"What time is it?" I asked.

"Six-thirty," Mom replied.

I got up and walked downstairs to the kitchen. Mom and Dad had a phone in their bedroom, but I didn't think they'd be too happy if I took the call in there. None of us got up before seven.

"They've called school off already," Margie said, after I'd mumbled hello at her. "I wanted to know if I should go out shoveling now, or wait until after breakfast."

"What are you talking about?" I asked her. My eyes were just starting to focus, and I wished I was still in the middle of my dream.

"The snow," she said. "Look out the window, Janie."

So I did. Everything was white.

"How can there be snow?" I asked. We had just had snow ten days ago.

"There's five inches," Margie declared. "Can I wait until after breakfast? I'm really hungry."

"Sure," I said. Executive decisions were easy if you were half asleep. "I'll see you in school."

"No school," Margie said. "Are you awake, Janie?"

"No," I told her and hung up. I made the long walk to my bedroom and climbed back into bed. No school meant I could sleep late. Carol would have to get up for her paper route, but there was no reason why I couldn't return to France for another couple of hours.

I had just drifted back to sleep when I had a vision of Herm shoveling his walk and dropping smack dead. It was so scary I woke right up and had to reassure myself that it had been nothing more than a dream.

I wasn't about to take any chances, though. It had been irresponsible of me to fall asleep in the first place. Herm's life was my sacred responsibility, and I had been willing to ignore it for the sake of a warm bed. I hated myself as I dressed swiftly for the job ahead. No wonder Dad kept telling me Kid Power was too much for me. How could I have forgotten Herm?

Sure enough, when I got my shovel over there, I found Herm standing at his door, looking the snow over. "Don't shovel!" I cried. "I'm here; I'll do it."

"You don't have to bother," he said. "There isn't that much. Shouldn't you be in school?"

"No school today," I said, starting to shovel frantically. Five more minutes and he probably would have been dead. Gert would never have forgiven me.

"Don't work so hard," Herm said, watching me shovel. "It isn't good to overwork your body like that."

I just grunted and shoveled. If he only knew how close he'd been to the grave, he wouldn't be so worried about my body. I swore never to forget Herm again. If it meant getting up at two in the morning, then so be it.

By the time I finished Herm's walk, I was exhausted. Not having eaten didn't help matters. I suddenly understood why Margie had called to ask about breakfast. Still, I had the driveway to go, and I could see Herm was itching to get at it. So I took a deep breath, and began clearing the snow.

Five inches isn't that much, but it was the heavy, wet kind of snow that weighs so much. It's the best snow for making snowmen and snowballs, but the worst for shoveling. And going at it at twice the speed of light didn't make things any easier. By the time I finished the driveway, I felt as if I'd run a marathon.

I went to the kitchen door, and Gert let me in. "I had a terrible time keeping Herm from shoveling," she told me as she handed me my money.

"I know. I'm sorry," I said. "It wasn't snowing when I went to bed last night. I didn't realize it had snowed, so I got a late start this morning. I swear I'll never be late again."

"I hope not," Gert said. "The whole idea was that you'd be nice and early so Herm wouldn't even think about shoveling."

There was no way of explaining to Gert that I felt bad enough without her scolding me. So I let her scold. I was cold and wet and famished, and a little extra scolding wasn't going to make me feel that much worse.

I yearned to go home and eat a warm, filling breakfast, but I figured I'd better do my other jobs first. So I walked over to Gail's house next and shoveled there. "I hope it doesn't keep snowing," she said, as she dug out the money from her pocketbook. "I'm a single parent, you know. Single parents don't have enough money for snow."

"I hope it doesn't snow much more either," I replied, not really meaning it. What I hoped was that it would only snow on the streets other kids were supposed to clear, and if it did snow on my streets as well, it would wait until about ten in the morning to stop. But that was too much to explain, so I just took the money and walked over to Mrs. Edwards's house.

I knew I could have waited until after breakfast to do her walk, but I was already shoveling. Besides, if her nurse's aide came first thing in the morning, it would be nice if the walk was already cleared for her. So I shoveled some more. Every muscle in my back and arms ached, and my stomach was growling, and my feet were soaking wet. Next time, Herm or no Herm, I was going to take the time to put on socks.

"Thank you for doing my walk," Mrs. Edwards said as she paid me. "But next time do you think you could shovel me a little sooner, Janie? My poor aide had to trudge here through the snow, and her feet got all wet."

"She's here already?" I asked.

"Oh, yes, she's very punctual," Mrs. Edwards said. "She shows up at eight on the dot, regardless of weather."

"I promise I'll get to you before eight, then," I said. Mrs. Edwards never asked things of me, so I felt terrible that I had let her down this time.

My last job was my own house. I was sure my parents would let me postpone the shoveling until after I'd eaten something. I pictured them waiting for me with the kitchen door wide open, the smells of pancakes and eggs and hot chocolate welcoming me home.

Instead I was greeted by my father standing at the front door. "There you are," he said. "I knew this was a lousy idea. Give me the shovel, and let me clear the driveway so I can get to work."

"I'll clear it, Dad," I said.

"I don't have time for that," he said. "Come on, Janie, let me do it."

Only I wouldn't let him. I just took the shovel and plowed through the driveway as fast as I possibly could. I was too angry to feel the pain. I tossed the snow into the air, and dug in farther, tossed and dug until there was space for the car to get out. Dad muttered thanks, and got into the car. I watched as he drove off, and then I cleared the sidewalk. There was no point not getting it done. My hot-breakfast fantasies had disappeared.

"I really wish you had done our driveway first," Mom told me as I plopped down on a kitchen chair. "Your father was very worried that he'd be late to work today. He had a very important meeting scheduled first thing, and he wasn't in that great a mood anyway, because of Margie's phone call."

"I had to do everybody else's walks, too," I said. "Next time I'll do our driveway first, and then I'll do the rest." Herm's heart would just have to wait. If he'd ever had a father, he'd understand.

"Carol's been on the phone all morning," Mom continued. "Your father wasn't too happy about that, either.

He thought there might be a call for him saying his meeting had been postponed or called off, but they wouldn't be able to reach him. He was really very angry by the time he left for work."

"I'm sorry," I said. "I'm sure this is the last snowfall of the year. Kid Power will probably stop existing by lunchtime. Then everybody will be happy."

"It's December tenth," Mom pointed out. "We can count on at least one snowfall in January and another in February, and probably one in March as well. And any one of those months could have two snowfalls, and we still have three weeks of December left to go. I suggest you work out the details for Kid Power before the next snowfall, or else your father may suggest you give up on the whole idea."

I sighed. "My feet are wet," I said. "Can I go upstairs now and put socks on?"

"You aren't wearing socks?" Mom asked. "You've been out shoveling snow with no socks on?"

"I didn't have time," I said, only it came out like a whine.

"You make the time, young lady," Mom said. "No amount of money is worth frostbite, or pneumonia. Do you want all that precious money you earn to go toward paying off doctor's bills?"

"I promise I'll do better," I said. "I promise I'll wake up in the middle of the night and shovel everybody's walk first thing. I'll wear three pairs of socks and two pairs of boots, and everybody will get to work on time."

"I don't care for that tone of voice, Janie," Mom said. "Go upstairs, take a warm bath, put on some dry clothes, and think about living up to your responsibilities."

"Yes, ma'am," I said. It took all my remaining strength just to get up from the chair. We only had five inches of snow, but I felt as if it had all fallen on me. I wondered if I drowned in the bathtub whether anybody would care enough to come to my funeral.

It took forever to get my feet warm, and by the time I did, I wasn't sure I wanted to risk going downstairs for breakfast. But I knew I'd have to face my mother again sometime, and it might as well be before I died of starvation.

So I walked downstairs, and went back to the kitchen. Mom was on the phone, doing Something Extra business, so I tried to make my breakfast as quietly as possible. It wasn't easy cracking eggs softly, but I tried. If Mom appreciated my effort, she didn't show it. Instead, she hung up from that call and made another.

I couldn't understand much of what she was saying, but it seemed to be about the birthday party for Elvira Butsworth. She'd seemed really excited about the idea when it first came up, but she had hardly mentioned it since then. I would have been happy for her that she was working on it again, except that I wasn't in the mood to be happy for anybody.

I scrambled the eggs so gently they practically came out as an omelet. Then I took the plate into the dining room to eat. I didn't see how I could make too much noise eating scrambled eggs, but I figured I'd taken my life into my own hands enough just by making breakfast. Mom didn't seem to be in the mood to listen to my swallowing and chewing.

"Where have you been?" Carol asked, as I finished the eggs. I was still hungry, but I didn't have enough nerve left to go back in the kitchen. Maybe I'd take some of the money I'd earned that morning and spend it on food.

"I was working," I said. "Shoveling people out. It snowed, you know."

"I'll say I know," Carol replied. "I had to call a million people to tell them to shovel. What a mess. Half the kids seemed to think that just because it was a snow day at school nobody had to go to work. They were all for staying in bed or making snowmen or just watching TV. I really had to do some fast talking to get them to their jobs."

"Thank you," I said, and meant it. If I'd had to do that as well as shovel, Kid Power would have died that morning.

"We do have one problem," Carol said. "Jeremy O'Shea recruited somebody for our senior citizen program. He wasn't quite sure what the man's name is; it starts with an *R*, and it has some *t*'s in it. In any event, the man just hated Jeremy, and Jeremy didn't much like him either, so he called me last week and said he was dropping him from his jobs. He'd stick to shoveling instead. I didn't bother telling you this last week because I figured it was my job to handle things like that."

"Thank you," I said again. Maybe Carol would be willing to handle everything if I asked her nicely enough.

"Anyway, I assigned this guy to Donna Manning," Carol continued. "Donna's a nice kid, and I figured she could get along with him better. Only she called me up two days later and begged to drop him. So I said sure, and asked Lisa if she'd mind switching old people. I mean senior citizens. Lisa gets along with everybody."

"So Mrs. Lucini doesn't have anybody anymore," I said.

"Oh, no," Carol said. "I gave Mrs. Lucini to Donna. They're getting along fine. But Lisa called me up in tears about an hour ago. She said she'd rather give up working altogether than have to keep on with this Mr. R. person. So I told her to calm down, that we'd find somebody else for her. She gave me this Mr. R. person's phone number, and I called him up as soon as I could, to see if I could convince him to drop out of the program. It wasn't easy, let me tell you, since I never did find out what his name was. Lisa calls him Mr. Rotten."

"Did he drop out?" I asked. Maybe he did and it would start a trend and everybody would drop out and I'd be able to retire. I didn't really need a computer. I still had most of my brain, after all.

"He refused to," Carol replied. "He said, and I quote, 'This Kid Power thing is a lousy idea, and I'm only doing it to keep my son off my back, but anything is worth it to keep that worrywart away from me. He thinks he knows everything, fat chance of that. You'd better find me a kid with a little respect for her elders, and a little bit of brain wouldn't hurt either, not that I'm expecting miracles.' So I figured you had a little bit of a brain, probably, and you do get along great with older people, and besides, you're the boss, so you should take on the hard jobs."

"What are you telling me, Carol?" I asked.

"Congratulations," Carol said, smiling broadly. "You won. Mr. Rotten is yours for the rest of the winter!"

Chapter

6

He was the tallest, skinniest, meanest-looking man I'd ever seen. Even his mustache looked mean. I wanted to run away from him before he even opened his mouth, but I stood at attention instead.

"So you're the new kid," he said. His teeth were yellow and mean-looking. "You got a name?"

"I'm Janie Golden," I said. "And I'm founder and president of Kid Power."

"Congratulations," he replied. "So this was all your stinking idea."

He was mostly bald. Maybe he'd been nicer before he lost his hair. My father says hair loss can be a real trauma. Or maybe he'd suffered some kind of terrible tragedy in his life. There were probably a lot of good reasons why he was as rotten as he was.

"I'm here to help you," I said. "If you want to go for a walk, or something. Or I can run errands for you." Maybe he wanted some errands done for him in China.

"A walk," he grunted. "Let me get my coat. I want to see all the snow on the ground."

"Okay," I said. That sounded like an almost human

statement. Maybe he was a snow lover. Maybe he missed being active in winter sports.

He came out bundled up in a heavy coat and carrying a cane. "Maybe we'll see some cars skidding around," he said with a chuckle. "Maybe there'll be an accident. Some kid sleds right into a car. Or some woman slips and lands right on her fanny in a snowdrift." He smacked his lips at the possibilities.

"Sounds like fun," I said. Mr. Rotten was obviously my punishment for not shoveling everybody's walk this morning before dawn. Not that I was convinced my character would improve from spending time with the man.

We walked around the block, and Mr. Rotten kept me entertained with his philosophy of life. "People stink," he said, peering around in search of an accident. "Everybody is out for number one. Nobody cares about anybody else. It's all me, me, me."

"People care," I said. "My father cares. I care."

"You're both in it for the money," Mr. Rotten replied. "What does your father do?"

"He's a labor lawyer," I replied.

"Biggest crooks of all," Mr. Rotten declared. "Except maybe for doctors and politicians. Plumbers, too. Hey, look at that."

So I looked. A little kid was sitting outside his front door, crying loudly and begging to be let back in. The door remained closed.

Mr. Rotten laughed hard. "Better learn now, kid," he said. "If you don't open the door for yourself, nobody is going to open it for you."

The kid just kept crying. I felt like joining him.

"What's your name again?" Mr. Rotten asked, as we walked away from the screaming kid.

"Janie," I said, although at this point I wished he didn't know.

"Life is a hellhole, Janie," Mr. Rotten said. "You like life?"

"Most of the time," I replied.

"You'll get over that," he said. "Soon enough you'll be sorry you were ever born."

I didn't think I'd have to wait very long.

"Get away, you lousy dog," Mr. Rotten said to a stray poodle. He swatted at it with his cane, and the dog ran off. I had hoped he'd lose his balance and I'd get to see him fall on the sidewalk, but he didn't waver once. He'd obviously had a lot of practice swatting at dogs.

"Life is a hellhole, and it's dog eat dog," Mr. Rotten continued. He kicked some snow into the face of a squirrel, which ran into traffic to escape. "You know who's the worst?"

"Lawyers?" I asked.

"Worse than lawyers, even," Mr. Rotten said. "Women. All women. They're what turns life into the stinkpot we're all stuck with."

"I am a girl," I said. "One of these days I'm going to be a woman."

"That's nothing to brag about, kid," Mr. Rotten said. "Women are the curse of all mankind."

"And vice versa, I'm sure," I replied. I couldn't believe this man. How had he managed to live so long without somebody murdering him?

"Human beings are all louses," Mr. Rotten declared, almost cheerfully. "Women are the biggest louses of all."

"I don't like you," I said. Why should he have any illusions?

"I didn't think you would," Mr. Rotten replied. "You going to quit taking me out for walks?"

"Absolutely not," I said. "It's my job, and I'll be here every day."

"We'll see about that," Mr. Rotten said, but at least he stopped talking for the rest of our walk. He snarled at cats and children, but by that point I felt like snarling right with him. Maybe he could give me snarling lessons.

We made it back safely to his house. He didn't ask me in, which was fine with me. "See you tomorrow?" he asked me.

"After school," I said.

"Maybe we'll be lucky," he said. "Maybe World War Three will happen tonight."

"I'll keep my fingers crossed," I replied, and gave him my biggest smile. As long as he knew I hated him, there was no reason not to be polite.

Mr. Rotten growled at me and went into his house. It was a nice house, too, very friendly-looking. There were geraniums in the window. Geraniums must be very hardy to survive in his atmosphere.

I walked home wondering what other bad things were going to happen that day. I figured my best bet was to have everything awful happen at once, so I could lead the rest of my life relatively happy. Otherwise World War Three would become a nice change of pace.

Carol was sitting in the living room reading a book. "I'm glad you're back," she said. "Something weird is going on."

I hung up my coat and went back to hear what it was. At that point, weird sounded positively pleasant.

"A couple of the kids called me to say they went out

this morning to shovel their walks," Carol began. "But when they got to the houses, they found that the walks were already cleared."

"Maybe they took too long to get there," I said. "A lot of people had to get out first thing this morning. They might have shoveled themselves out."

"That's what I thought," Carol said. "After all, you're not the only lazy member of Kid Power."

"Get to the point, Carol," I said.

"Well, the kids went to the houses to see what had happened," Carol said. "And they were all told that Kid Power had already been there to shovel."

"What?" I asked, sitting up straight.

"The people at all the houses said that kids showed up first thing this morning and shoveled the walks," Carol continued. "And then they went to the house and said Kid Power had sent them to shovel, and that our fee had gone up to five dollars. The people were all very upset, but apparently they all paid, since their walks and drive-ways had been cleared. But they were angry that the rates had gone up without anybody telling them."

"We couldn't tell them," I said. "Our rates haven't gone up."

"Tell that to the unsuspecting public," Carol said. "I got four phone calls about it from kids. They were upset that somebody stole their jobs from them."

"I don't believe any of this," I said. "I retire. Kid Power is all yours."

"You mean it?" Carol asked, a little too eagerly.

"No," I said, as soon as I saw the glint in her eyes. Maybe I could fix her up with Mr. Rotten. They'd be perfect together.

"I got the names of all the people it happened to," Carol said. "Our customers' names, I mean. You might want to give them a call and explain what happened."

"But I don't know what happened," I said. "How can I explain?"

Carol shrugged. "That's why you're the executive," she said. "Because you think so fast on your feet."

My feet were still cold from that morning. And I was developing a headache the size of Mount Rushmore. "Do you have any ideas about what's going on?" I asked Carol.

"Somebody is trying to steal our business," she replied. "And it sounds as if he's doing a good job of it."

"Johnny Richards," I said.

"That's my guess," she replied.

"That really stinks," I said. "Dad gave me this whole speech about the open marketplace and the value of competition and price wars, but he didn't say a thing about people just stealing other people's business."

"He doesn't know Johnny," Carol said.

"I wish I didn't," I said. "What do you think we should do?"

"You mean what *you* should do," Carol said. "I'm just an underpaid flunky."

Maybe Mr. Rotten was right about the world. What he said certainly pertained to older sisters. "Okay," I said with a sigh. "What should I do?"

"I don't know," Carol said. "If I knew answers to questions like that, I'd be an executive, and not just an underpaid flunky."

"I hate you," I told her. I hated everybody just then, but Carol was my most convenient target. "You're a terrible older sister. You don't try to help at all. You don't love me. All you love is money. I'll bet you and Johnny got together and came up with the idea of stealing Kid Power away from me. Well, the two of you can have it. I never want to see you again." I stormed out of the room and ran upstairs to my bedroom. I slammed my door so hard that three pencils rolled off my desk.

I didn't bother picking them up. Instead I lay flat on my bed and cried. This was the worst day of my life. My parents were both mad at me, my customers all hated me, even Mrs. Edwards had sort of scolded me, I'd had to deal with the foulest man in the Western Hemisphere, Kid Power was being stolen from me, and nobody cared one little bit. As far as they were all concerned, my universe could collapse and they'd just laugh.

Not to mention my cold feet and empty stomach. I was in a state of total misery for almost twenty minutes. I would have stayed there considerably longer if Carol hadn't knocked on my door.

"Phone call for you," she said.

"Who?" I asked her, grabbing some tissues and blowing my nose loudly. Let her witness my misery. It was partly her fault, after all.

"Mrs. Schmidt," Carol said. "She's one of Terry Miller's customers."

"Thank you," I said, heaving a sigh. I got off my bed and walked to my parents' room to use their phone. "Hello, Mrs. Schmidt," I said. "What can I do for you?"

"I'm calling to compliment you on the lovely job you did on my walk," Mrs. Schmidt said. "Your boy shoveled me out so well there's hardly a trace of snow left. I'm going to tell all my friends about Kid Power. I'm sure you'll get lots of extra business."

"Thank you," I said, feeling a little better about things. At least somebody still appreciated Kid Power. "I'll tell Terry you called."

"Is that the boy's name?" Mrs. Schmidt asked.

"Terry's a girl," I said. You'd think she would have noticed that.

"Oh, then, there must be some mistake," Mrs. Schmidt said. "My walk was definitely shoveled by a boy."

"A boy," I said. There were a thousand possible explanations. Terry might have sent a boy over to shovel. Carol could have been wrong about whose customer Mrs. Schmidt was. Mr. Rotten might have shoveled the walk to prove he really wasn't that bad a person. I might still be dreaming and this whole day had never happened. "How much did this boy charge you, Mrs. Schmidt?"

"Five dollars," Mrs. Schmidt replied. "I thought I was supposed to pay a little less than that, but he was certainly worth the extra money. And to be perfectly honest, when I agreed to let Kid Power shovel my walk, I wasn't paying all that much attention to details. It was very possible the figure was five dollars and I just didn't hear right. In any event, I'll be delighted to keep on paying the five dollars if you'll promise me that the same boy will shovel my walk."

The worst day of my life had just grown a little worse. "I'm glad you were satisfied with our work," I said, even though it wasn't our work she was satisfied with. "Thank you for calling, Mrs. Schmidt."

"Thank you," Mrs. Schmidt said. "And you can be sure I'll tell all my friends."

"Good bye," I said, and hung up the phone. I wiped the tears off my cheek. Not only was Johnny Richards stealing all Kid Power's business, but his friends were better at their jobs than we were. Nobody had called to praise any of us for our work.

I went back to my bedroom and closed my door, too upset to slam it. I crawled back into bed, pulled the covers over my head, and waited for the sobs to start again.

But they didn't. Instead, I started getting mad. Here I was, trying to run an organization that gave work to a lot of deserving kids and saved the lives of people who might otherwise lose them from careless shoveling, and all I got was aggravation and complaints. Kid Power might singlehandedly save a half-dozen people from slipping on the ice that winter and breaking their ankles or legs or hips or backs, and nobody would even think to thank us. I was surrounded by the basest sort of ingratitude.

If that was what Johnny wanted, then he could have it, I decided. Let him take Mr. Rotten out for his daily walk. Let him shovel the walks of twenty-five people at the same time. Let him get cold feet and no food for a few miserable dollars. As far as I was concerned, Kid Power was his for the taking.

The first person I decided to announce my decision to was Lisa. She had never liked Kid Power, so she was bound to be happy that I'd decided to give it up. I put on my boots and my coat and sneaked out of the house. It was amazing that after such a long day, there was still daylight left. But there was, and when I reached Lisa's house, I found her outside throwing snowballs at her little brother Stevie. So I joined in. We missed each other more often than we made a direct hit, but that was okay, too. Just throwing the snow around felt good.

After we'd finished with the snowballs, we made tiny snowpeople. There wasn't enough snow on the ground for a full-sized snowman, so we made miniatures instead. Stevie is usually a pest, but he was so happy we were playing with him that he behaved okay. And I enjoyed doing something with snow other than shoveling it.

Lisa's housekeeper had hot chocolate and cookies waiting for us when we went inside. That was the warmest I'd felt all day, and certainly the happiest. I'd had fun, for a change, and I was about to give up all my responsibilities and return to life as a normal kid. Things were going to be okay from then on.

"Guess what I've decided to do," I told Lisa, as we took some extra cookies to her bedroom.

"I give up," Lisa said. Lisa isn't very good at guessing.

"I've decided to give up Kid Power," I told her triumphantly. "I'm going to let Johnny Richards take it over. He wants it more than I do these days."

"You can't do that," Lisa said. "You can't give up Kid Power. It's your life."

"It is not my life," I replied.

"Well, you created it," Lisa said. "And you've worked so hard for months to make it into a success. You don't just give up something like that because a mood hits you."

"The mood wasn't what hit me," I said. "Besides, I thought you'd be happy. You're always telling me what a mistake Kid Power is."

"I don't think Kid Power is a mistake," Lisa said. "Just when you get carried away with it. But this winter it's very different. You've listened to my complaints, and you've hired Carol to help out, and I know the other kids are happy to have a chance to earn money. You owe it to everybody to keep Kid Power going forever. Besides, I thought you wanted the computer."

"I do," I said. "But maybe my parents will buy one for me."

"That really makes me mad," Lisa said. "I thought you were willing to work for what you wanted. I didn't realize you were the sort of person who just waited for somebody else to get it for you."

"I'm twelve years old," I pointed out. "I don't exactly support myself. My parents pay for my food and my clothes, and if they're willing to pay for my computer, then that's okay, too. I don't understand you at all, Lisa. All you ever do is complain about Kid Power. You never say anything good about it. And now when I've finally decided to get rid of it, you don't tell me what a great thing I'm doing. You just scold me some more. I'm tired of being scolded. I've been scolded all day. Why don't you just say you're happy I've decided to give Kid Power up and let it go at that? What kind of a friend are you?"

"I'm your best friend," Lisa said. "And I want you to be happy. I just don't think you're going to be happy giving Kid Power up like this. That's all. If you don't understand that, then I'm real sorry."

"I understand," I said. "I understand that if I want support for my decision, I'd better go home and talk with my family. They really hate Kid Power. They're bound to agree with me, no matter what you think."

"Fine," Lisa said. "Go home. I'll see you in school tomorrow."

"If World War Three doesn't happen first," I replied, and got up, grabbing an extra cookie for the walk home. Suddenly I felt a real need for nourishment.

Carol was setting the table when I got home, and Mom was taking supper out of the oven. "Oh, good," Mom said when she saw me. "Supper's just about ready. Wash your hands, and join us at the table."

So I did what she said. Dinner smelled great, and I had a huge appetite, in spite of Lisa's cookies.

"This has been such a great day," Mom said as we all sat down. "You know how I've been working on an idea for Something Extra. Well, the snow inspired me. I've decided to throw Elvira Butsworth a winter carnival party. It was all the snow on the ground that made me think of it. I was on the phone all morning checking things out with people, and everybody agrees it's a great idea."

"It does sound good," Dad said. "A winter carnival is something the whole town can get involved in."

"That's it exactly," Mom said, helping herself to some broccoli. "Carol's idea about getting the schools involved seemed so sensible to me, but I didn't know how to put it together with old Elvira. Now I think we'll have school competitions. The best ice sculpture of Elvira, the most creative posters, that sort of thing. Maybe we'll hold racing events at the carnival. I'll need to get all sorts of permits and cooperation, but at least I have the idea. And I have a slogan, too. I'm going to put an ad in the paper saying, 'Something Extra for Elvira Butsworth.' That should get people thinking, don't you think? Then as the details get worked out, I'll send out press releases."

"Or hold a press conference," Dad said. "Get people from the newspapers and the radio station and cable TV to come, and then you can get even more publicity."

Mom smiled. "Of course I'll expect you guys to do a little more than usual around here while I'm setting all this up," she said. "I'm hoping to have the carnival on the Sunday after the Super Bowl in January. No point competing with the Super Bowl."

"It sounds perfect," Dad said. "Let me know what I can do to help."

"I can help around the house a lot," I said. This was the perfect opportunity to tell them my news. "I've decided to give up Kid Power."

"What?" Carol said.

"You heard me," I said. "I've decided to give up Kid Power."

"But I was just bragging about you today," Dad said. "I was telling everybody at the meeting this morning about my daughters and how they're running a large organization and still living up to their responsibilities. Everybody at that meeting was late, except for me, and they were all tired and grouchy from shoveling their walks. But not me. I said Janie had done it, and what's more she'd organized a lot of the school kids to shovel walks all over town, and Carol was in charge of personnel. They were all quite impressed. A couple of the people even wanted to talk to Janie, to see if she could suggest ways they could get their kids to start an organization like Kid Power."

Nobody could drive me crazy quite as fast as my father could. "You're always telling me to quit Kid Power," I said. "Why do you brag about it to other people and then complain to me about it?"

"Because I have mixed feelings about it," Dad said. "This morning, for example, I was feeling very rushed, and I don't like driving on snowy streets, so I wasn't looking forward to the drive, and I wasn't too thrilled about that first-thing-in-the-morning phone call you got. I took it all out on you, and I'm sorry. I owe you an apology. But I've always felt that if you can manage Kid Power and everything else in your life, then of course you should keep it going. I hope you didn't decide to give it up just because I was in a bad mood this morning."

"No," I said. "There are a lot of other reasons."

"I hope I'm not one of them," Carol said. "I know you were mad at me this afternoon, but I hope that isn't the reason you've decided to give Kid Power up."

"Not completely," I said.

"Sometimes it's hard for me to come up with ideas

to help," Carol said. "Especially if you ask me before I've had time to think about it. But I never wanted you to give up Kid Power."

"Of course not," I said. "Not when you can earn money from it."

"Sure, I like earning money," Carol said. "But I don't need Kid Power for that. I have my newspaper route, and my baby-sitting. I liked helping out with Kid Power because it was a different way of working. Besides, I sort of enjoyed working with you. Sometimes. Maybe not this afternoon, but other times I've really liked it."

"You all make me sick!" I cried. "All I wanted was a little support because I've decided to give up Kid Power, but instead you act as if Kid Power is the greatest thing ever invented. Well, what about me? Don't I count for more than Kid Power?" Before they had a chance to answer, I got up and ran out of the dining room and up to my bedroom. I felt as if I'd spent half the day running to my bedroom, and getting there never made me feel any better.

I was sitting on my bed congratulating myself on having cheated myself out of another meal when there was a knock on my door. The day had started with a knock on the door, and things had gone straight downhill from there. Maybe the answer was to take down the door.

"Can I come in?" Mom asked. "I'd like to talk with you, Janie, if you don't mind."

"Come on in," I said. Mom hadn't said anything at the table. Maybe she was here to tell me giving up Kid Power was one smart idea. Anything was possible.

Mom sat down on the bed next to me, and then she put her arm around me. I cuddled next to her. It felt real good to sit that way.

"First of all, we all want you to know we love you," Mom said. "And none of us meant to upset you, which we've obviously done all day. Are we forgiven?"

"Sure," I said.

"Now, I don't know what's going on with Kid Power, but I do want to say something," Mom continued. "Your father and I and Carol, too, are very proud of what you've done with Kid Power. And I have to admit I loved the idea of my two girls working together. I probably put too much pressure on you to take Carol on. It certainly wasn't your idea, and it's possible you really didn't want to work with Carol but felt you had to."

I shook my head. "It was okay working with Carol," I said. "I like Carol most of the time."

Mom laughed. "That's pretty good for sisters your age," she said, holding me even closer. "Now I want to say something very selfish. I don't want you to quit Kid Power. For my sake, I want you to stay with it."

"Why?" I asked.

"Because you're a real inspiration for me," Mom said. "Here I am, trying to get a brand-new business going, and sometimes the jobs don't come in, or the workers don't do the job they promised me they would, or there are simply problems I can't come up with solutions to, and I want to scream. I used to have such a nice job. I did my work, and I got my paycheck, and I wasn't responsible for anybody else's work. But with Something Extra, I have to run it all, and if it's a failure, it's my failure. Of course its success is my success, too, but I have a long way to go before I can feel any security about it."

"Something Extra is going to be a big success," I told her. "We all know that."

"I'm glad you do," Mom said. "Sometimes I don't, and that's when I think about Kid Power and everything you've done with it. The day we bought you your bike may have been the proudest day of my life. You knew what you wanted, and you figured out a way of getting it all on your own. And I tell myself you had to have gotten that strength and intelligence from somebody, and just maybe it was me. If you can do it, then I can do it, too. I just hope I can derive half as much pride from Something Extra as I do from Kid Power."

"Oh, Mom," I said, and buried my head in her shoulder.

"You've obviously had an awful day," Mom said, patting me on my head. "And I know I was responsible for some of it, and your father was responsible, too, and maybe Carol was, also. But we all want to hear what your reasons are for giving up Kid Power. Because if there's any way we can help you keep it going, if you decide you want to do that, then we sure want to do what we can. And if you decide after talking to us that you really do want to give Kid Power up, then all of us will support your decision. All right?"

"All right," I said.

"Are you willing to come back down to dinner?" Mom asked. "I put your plate in the oven so your food wouldn't get cold."

"Thank you," I said. "I am hungry."

"Good," Mom said. "Come on, then. Let's find out just what's going on here."

I followed Mom downstairs. Dad and Carol were still sitting at the table. It looked as if they'd barely touched their food. I took my plate out of the oven and joined them. We all ate silently for a few minutes, and then I explained to all of them about Herm's heart and Mr. Rotten's personality, and Mrs. Schmidt's phone call, and Johnny Richards and what he was doing to Kid Power.

"So I figured I'd just give it to Johnny," I said. "If he's going to steal it away from me, he might as well just have it. Besides, he does a better job than we can do, so he deserves to have it. If he wants to work with Carol, that's fine with me."

"Hold on one second," Carol said. "I have no intention of working with a creep like Johnny Richards. Working with you is tough enough, but at least you're a human being."

"So don't work with Johnny," I said, shrugging. "That's your decision, not mine."

"Calm down, both of you," Dad said. "Janie, you made a lot of statements that I don't think you've really thought out."

"Like what?" I challenged him.

"For example, you said that Johnny is doing a better job than you are," Dad explained. "You don't know that. You don't even know for sure that it was Johnny who shoveled Mrs. Schmidt's walk. Maybe he's trying to organize his friends the way you organized Kid Power."

"I guess that's possible," I said. "But even that way, I'm in trouble. So his friends do a better job than mine. What difference does that make?"

"It makes a lot of difference," Dad said. "For starters, if you're really worried that your friends aren't doing quality work, then you can tell them to do better. You can fire the ones who don't. You can check with the people whose walks they cleared to see if they're satisfied. Don't forget, you're charging less than Johnny is, and that counts for something, too."

"Carol can fire them," I said. "She's in charge of personnel."

"Great," Carol said. "I've always wanted to fire people."

Dad shuddered. "For another thing," he said, "you can see if Johnny's friends might be willing to work with Kid Power instead of for Johnny. You don't know the kind of terms he's offering them. They might take a pay cut for better working conditions."

"Like working for human beings," Carol said.

"But even if I do all that, what if Johnny continues to steal my clients?" I asked. "Then where am I?"

"There are some advantages to having a labor lawyer for a father," Dad said. "If the only reason you want to give up Kid Power is because you think you're going to lose it to Johnny, then I'll happily teach you negotiation techniques. That way you can confront Johnny and work out your differences peaceably and successfully. What do you say?"

I thought about it. Kid Power certainly did mean a lot to me. And I had to admit I was pleased it meant a lot to my family and to Lisa, also. Besides, it wasn't fair that a bully like Johnny could get what I'd worked so hard at because he was willing to cheat and steal.

"You're on, Dad," I said. "Teach me how to negotiate Johnny Richards into a quivering mass of pulp."

"It'll be my pleasure," Dad said, and for the first time that day everybody in my family laughed.

Chapter 8

I assigned to Carol the job of collecting all our ten percents, and cornered Johnny on my own as we were walking toward the cafeteria. "I have to talk with you," I told him in my best no-nonsense voice. "Be firm and calm," Dad had told me the night before. "Make him realize you're the one in control of the situation."

That certainly wasn't how I felt, but I figured it was like whistling when you were afraid; if you faked him out, you faked yourself out as well. At least I hoped that was how it worked. I felt like whistling just to drown out the sound of my knees knocking.

"I figured you might want to," Johnny said. "Mind if my friends join us?"

I checked out Johnny's friends. They were three of the biggest, toughest boys in our school district. They probably got together and compared broken noses and knocked-out teeth. If I was scared of Johnny, I was petrified of his friends.

"Don't show fear or uncertainty," my father had told me. "If Johnny makes a request or a demand that you can't accept, just say so."

So I said no. Only I wasn't sure Johnny would know what I meant. "I mean no, I don't want your friends to join us," I said, feeling dumb. My only hope was that Johnny was dumb, too, and wouldn't realize I was dumber.

"If that's how you feel," Johnny said. He snapped his fingers, and his friends actually vanished. At least they left quietly and without protest. I only wished my friends would be that cooperative. Maybe I could get Johnny to give me some pointers.

I followed Johnny to a table in an out-of-the-way corner of the cafeteria. He put his brown-bag lunch on the table, but I continued to hold mine. I figured I might have a psychological advantage if he was chewing and I wasn't. Dad had told me to seize on any advantage I could get. Dad was obviously a great negotiator.

Johnny unwrapped his sandwich and took a big bite out of it. He smiled at me as he chewed. I just stared. If I smiled and chewed like that, my mother would be all over me for bad table manners.

"You stole some of Kid Power's business," I said, remembering finally to seize the advantage.

"What if I did?" Johnny asked, his mouth full of tuna salad.

"I can't let you keep doing that to me," I told him.

"What are you planning to do about it?" he asked, almost curiously. Judging from the way he continued to demolish his sandwich, he wasn't overly concerned.

It was a good thing Dad had given me such a thorough training session the night before. Otherwise I might have panicked. Instead I just called Johnny's bluff. "We have ways of making you stop," I told him.

"Yeah?" he asked. "Like what?"

"I'm not going to tell you," I said. "Jeez. What kind of fool do you take me for?"

"What kind of fool are you?" he asked. "I wouldn't want to take you for the wrong kind."

"Why do you want to steal our business?" I asked. "There's plenty of work for both of us."

"I don't like your attitude," Johnny replied, and shoved the rest of his sandwich into his mouth. "The way you and your little friends just took our jobs away from us. I can't let you get away with that sort of thing."

"We didn't take anything," I said. "We just got organized before you did."

"We never had to get organized," Johnny said, wiping tuna salad off his face with the back of his hand. "When it snowed, we'd go out and shovel. Nothing fancy. Yesterday, by the time we got outside, half the walks were shoveled already. Kid Power got there first. There was hardly anything left for us to do. We had no choice but to tell people we were Kid Power. Believe me, it was embarrassing to have to say it. But a man's got to do what a man's got to do."

"So does a girl," I said. "There's no law that says you get dibs on walks. I went from door to door selling Kid Power's services. I'm not about to give up that business just because it makes you unhappy."

"It makes my friends unhappy, too," he said. "I don't think you want to make my friends unhappy, do you?"

"I don't want to make anybody unhappy," I said. "And that includes all of Kid Power's employees. You want to throw seventeen kids out of work just so you and your friends will be happy?" Dad would be proud of me.

"Certainly not," Johnny said. "I'm no monster, Golden. I just want what's fair."

"Fine," I said. "What's fair is you respect Kid Power's territory."

"That's not exactly how I see it," Johnny replied. "Kid Power didn't respect my territory, after all."

"I'm sure we can compromise," I said. Dad had told me not to be afraid to offer a compromise, just as long as I had control over the terms and didn't give up anything I was unwilling to let go of.

"Compromise," Johnny said, pursing his lips thoughtfully. He had some tuna salad left on the corner of his mouth. I yearned to wipe it off, along with his smirk. "Okay, Golden, let's talk compromise."

"You leave Kid Power alone," I said. "And tell us what houses you always used to shovel. We'll let you keep those, and you let us keep the others we've gotten."

"No," Johnny said.

Johnny obviously didn't understand negotiation. "What do you mean no?" I said. "I offered you a compromise. You can't just turn it down."

"Why not?" Johnny asked. "Oh, that's right. You have ways of making me do things." He smiled broadly.

"All right," I said. "You heard my offer. What do you want?" Dad had told me to be willing to listen to what Johnny wanted. I shouldn't automatically say no just because I hated his guts.

"It isn't a question of what I want," Johnny said. "It's what I'm going to have. Me and my friends are going to shovel just as many walks as we want to. If we have to say we're from Kid Power, then we'll say it. I don't suppose you got many complaints about our work yesterday."

"People weren't happy about paying more than they'd agreed to pay," I told him.

"But they paid it," Johnny replied. "Face it, Golden, my friends and me do superior work. We deserve superior pay. You should be grateful we're using your dumb name. It reflects well on you."

"I'll live without the reflection," I said. "Don't say you're from Kid Power anymore, Johnny."

"You don't seem to understand," Johnny said. "I'll say whatever I want to say. My friends will say whatever they want. There's nothing you can do to stop us. You'll be a lot happier once you understand that, Golden."

I would have kicked him in the shins, but Dad had told me not to stoop to Johnny's level.

"But I don't like to make little girls cry," Johnny continued, even though I was not about to cry. I'd cried enough the day before to last me until college. "So I'll tell you what I'll do for you."

"What?" I asked, in spite of myself. Maybe Johnny had decided to move to a different state. There were forty-nine others to make miserable, after all. Why should he think small?

"Kid Power does other stuff, right?" Johnny said. "More than shoveling."

"What of it?" I asked.

"You help old people cross streets," he said. "Regular bunch of Boy Scouts. Well, me and my friends don't care about that stuff. The pay isn't good enough to make us hang out with old people. I hate old people. They give me the creeps. You and your little friends can play with the old people all you like, Now, isn't that nice of us?"

"You're a real sweetheart," I said.

"My ma says the same thing," Johnny said, smiling cheerfully. "Do we understand ourselves now, Golden? My friends and I shovel as much as we want, the whole darn town if we want — calling ourselves Kid Power or the Republican party or anything we want, and if we leave a walk or two unshoveled, well, be our guests. And you can walk your old people, and scoop up after your doggies, and play Santa's helpers all you want. Those are my terms, and now they're your terms, too. That's my compromise. You do like it, don't you, Golden?"

I bit my lip, trying to think of what to say. I wished Dad was there to negotiate for me; he was bound to do a better job than I was doing.

"I'm glad you agree," Johnny said. "I could see you were a smart kid. Maybe someday we'll even go out together, once you get a little bigger in all the important places."

"You are a sleaze," I told him. "I wouldn't go out with you if my mother's life depended on it. And I haven't agreed to anything, not to any of your terms."

"I'm sorry to hear it," Johnny said. "But you're going to be sorrier."

"That's where you're wrong," I said. "You're the one who's going to be sorry. When I say we have ways, I mean it. And you're not going to like them one bit. So I'll give you one more chance, out of the incredible goodness of my heart, to lay off Kid Power. This is it, Johnny. Say yes now, or be prepared to be sorry later."

"I'm prepared," Johnny said. "I hope you are, too. Because if this means war, then only one of us is going to come out alive. And the smart money is on me."

It probably was, too. "You have tuna fish on your chin," I informed him as I got up from the table. My one triumph was watching him automatically wipe his chin with his hand. It wasn't triumph enough.

I spent the rest of the school day getting madder and madder. It drove me crazy that I hadn't managed to get what I wanted. I'd made Johnny a perfectly reasonable offer. I'd even been prepared to negotiate further. I'd offered to let him keep the jobs he'd stolen from us if he guaranteed not to take any more away. Instead I'd been given our town's old people and doggy concessions. The injustice of it made me want to scream.

Instead I tried to think of ways of stopping Johnny, and I started to gear myself up for another fun session with Mr. Rotten. There was always the chance that I had exaggerated Mr. Rotten's personality flaws. Yesterday had been a terrible day. Maybe Mr. Rotten was a lot nicer than I imagined and he was just picking up on my bad mood. It was nice to have something to hope for.

"So you actually came back," Mr. Rotten said when he opened the door for me. "I'll say one thing for you. You're persistent. Stupid and persistent."

I considered pointing out that that was two things, but I decided it would be bad manners. "Do you want to go for a walk?" I asked instead.

"Sure. Why not?" Mr. Rotten growled. "Wait there, dummy, while I get my coat."

So I waited. I had never in my entire life let anybody call me dummy, not even Carol. And here this stranger was calling me that and worse, and I was standing in the cold just so I could take him for a walk. If I'd had my way that day, there would have been two pairs of kicked shins in town.

"This is one lousy day," Mr. Rotten declared as we started our stroll. "TV reception stank. Not that there was anything good to watch anyway. Never is. But I pay good money for my cable, and the least I should get is good reception for the lousy shows they put on the air."

"Umph," I said. All he deserved was an occasional umph.

"My stupid daughter-in-law drops by in the afternoon," Mr. Rotten continued. "Am I okay? Do I need anything? I need her to leave me alone, but nothing stops that one. She's full of airs, that one. Hey, look at that!"

In spite of myself, I looked. A woman was slipping on an icy spot, grabbing hold of a parked car in an effort to keep from falling. The harder she fought to maintain her balance, the harder Mr. Rotten laughed. When she finally fell down, he laughed so hard I was ashamed to be seen standing next to him. So I ran over to the woman to see if I could help her.

"I'm all right," she said, grabbing her packages. "The only thing that's bruised is my dignity."

So I walked back to Mr. Rotten. "I don't like that, kid," he told me. "You're being paid to walk me, not run to the rescue of every nut who falls down on the street."

"Forgive me," I said. "I didn't mean to be a decent human being in your presence."

"Think you're so smart," Mr. Rotten said. "Don't you, you dumb kid."

There was no point even trying to talk. I just went back to umphing. Fortunately nobody else slipped during our walk. There were no accidents, no abandoned children. Not even a dog for Mr. Rotten to swing his cane at. I could see he was disappointed, which was fine by me.

"See you tomorrow?" he asked me, as he unlocked his door.

"Umph," I said. Let him figure out what that meant.

"Umph to you, too, sucker," he said, and slammed the door in my face. So I stuck my tongue out at him. It wasn't much, but it was all I had.

"Well, I hope your day was better than mine," Mom said, as I entered the kitchen.

"I don't see how it could have been," I said. "Why? What went wrong with yours?"

"I tried to speak to the mayor," Mom said. "Or at least make an appointment to speak to the mayor. You wouldn't think that would be so hard. This is not a big city, Janie. It's not the smallest town in the world, but it certainly isn't a big city, either. It shouldn't be that hard to get to speak to the mayor. But she was never in. She was at a meeting, or she was out to lunch, or she was taking care of a family matter, or she was at another meeting. I spent half the day on hold."

"That is aggravating," I said, getting myself an apple from the refrigerator.

"I finally reached her half an hour ago," Mom continued. "And I told her my plan, or as much of it as she let me tell her. But before I got halfway through with it, she said she had grave reservations about the whole idea. We'd be making a mockery of the memory of Elvira Butsworth. What was Something Extra, anyway? Competition between the schools would just divide the town, not unite it. I mean, the silliest reasons you can imagine for refusing to hear me out. I finally got her to allow me the chance to write her a proposal, and she said she'd get to it when she had a chance. I know it's still early December, but she sounded as if she'd take forever. I want to have the winter carnival in the winter. Ice skating is no fun on water."

"Maybe she'll read the proposal right away," I said. "It is a good idea, and she's bound to realize that once she does read it."

"I love you, Janie," Mom said. "Now all I have to do is find out how to spell her name. Rhazhnophski. What a mouthful."

"It'll all work out," I told Mom with a lot more confidence than I felt. The way the world looked to me just then, nothing was ever going to work out for the Golden family again.

Chapter 9

"So how did it go?" Dad asked that night at supper. I'd been afraid he'd ask, and had decided not to tell him the exact, unvarnished truth. Why make him feel bad, just because he didn't know how to negotiate with a nonhuman sleaze?

"Okay, I guess," I replied. "We had a quiz in English, but I think I did all right."

"That wasn't what I meant," he said. "How did your talk go with Johnny?"

"Oh, that," I said. "We talked for a while at lunch."

"And were you able to reach an accord?" Dad asked.

"I don't know if I'd call it an accord," I said. "Mom, could I please have the peas?"

"Sure," Mom said, passing them to me.

I helped myself to some peas, spooning them onto my plate very carefully. Peas can be tricky if you don't give them your fullest concentration. I only hoped Dad realized that.

"Negotiations frequently take more than one day," Dad said, watching me and the peas. "Of course, the more serious the situation, the longer it can take. And if the two sides are very far apart in their demands, it can take weeks, even months, before an accord is reached."

"It had better not take weeks," Carol said. "Snow doesn't last forever."

"It won't take weeks," I told her.

"Were you and Johnny able to reach agreement on the major issues?" Dad asked.

"That's kind of hard to say," I replied, and then filled my mouth with peas, to make it even harder.

"But you did make progress," Dad said. "The two of you talked, and you told each other where you stand. Even that is a help when you're negotiating. And you were firm with him, right? No nonsense, but nonviolent."

"Definitely," I said.

"Only so much negotiating can be done in a lunch hour," Dad said. "Professional negotiators sometimes lock themselves up in a room together for days to reach agreement."

"I refuse to be locked in a room with Johnny Richards," I said.

"Nobody is suggesting that," Mom said. "The important thing is that you're both trying."

"And that you're willing to ask an expert for advice," Dad said. "An important thing for you girls to realize is that there's no shame in asking someone for help. Especially when it's a field you don't know that much about. I was very flattered that Janie turned to me for advice, and I'm always available if either of you—or you, Meg— needs advice on a legal matter."

"We'll keep that in mind, Art," Mom said, smiling at him.

"I'm being pompous," Dad said. "All right, I'll keep my mouth shut for the rest of dinner."

That was fine with me, just as long as he didn't expect me to open mine. Instead I concentrated on the peas, and let Carol and Mom hold up everyone else's end of the conversation.

Carol cornered me as I was going to bed. "Let's talk," she said, following me into my room.

My sister never wants to talk with me, so I immediately got nervous.

"It didn't go well with you and Johnny, did it?" she asked.

"Not very," I admitted. "Johnny's idea of negotiating is to demand whatever he wants."

"I just want to say that I'll help anyway I can," Carol declared. "I'm on your side on this one."

"Thanks," I said, not pointing out that my side was Carol's side. Never alienate an ally. I was sure Dad had told me that at some point in his negotiation lecture.

"It may even work out someday," Carol said. "Johnny may lose interest in shoveling after a while. Or maybe he'll get arrested for something."

"I don't think we should count on it," I said. "But thanks for the thought."

"Let me know what I can do," Carol said, and for a moment she stared at me. Then she gave me a quick kiss on the forehead. I don't know which one of us was more surprised.

"'Night," she mumbled, and left my room fast.

"'Night," I replied. Carol wasn't just my ally. She was my friend, my sister. Who would have thought it?

It was nice having Carol on my side, but that wasn't

the solution to my problem. Having Dad on my side hadn't helped much, either. My best bet, I figured, was that it wouldn't snow for a while, long enough at least for me to work out a solution. That shouldn't take more than two or three years.

"How're things going?" Lisa asked me before school began. We were walking toward our lockers. I was watching out for Johnny, hoping not to see him.

"Okay," I said.

"You settle things with Johnny?" she persisted.

"Not exactly," I said. "I think he thinks things are settled, but I don't."

"I hope you can work things out," Lisa continued. "I was real happy you decided to keep Kid Power going."

"I know," I said. I still didn't understand, but I knew.

"Anyway, if there's anything I can do to help, let me know," Lisa said.

"I will," I said, feeling a little better. It was good to know that people cared about me. I just wished I knew how they could help.

The school day trudged along. I spent more time trying to figure out a solution to my problems than I did on my schoolwork, but none of my teachers called on me, so I got away with it. If I flunked all my classes, it would be Johnny's fault, I decided, but I knew my parents wouldn't see it that way.

"Hey, Golden."

In spite of myself, I turned at the sound of my name. I knew it was Johnny, and I knew I didn't want to talk to him, and I turned away.

"Wait up," he said, so I did. The school day had just ended, and I was on my way to my locker to get my coat.

"Have a nice day?" he asked me.

"Nice enough," I said. Dad had told me to keep the lines of communication open, but I didn't want them to be too open. "Why?"

"I figured you'd like a day when it didn't snow," Johnny said. "Maybe you'd talk your family into moving to Florida. Mexico, maybe."

"We're not moving anywhere," I said.

"Oh, that's right," Johnny said. "You have ways of making me stop. Care to tell me what those ways are?"

"I'm not about to tell you," I said. "But take it from me. You'll be sorry you didn't agree to a compromise."

"I can't wait to hear what those ways are," Johnny said. "Let me know as soon as you can, okay, Golden?"

"Oh, you'll know," I said. "I won't have to tell you."

"Should be fun," Johnny said, and started walking away from me.

I felt like a total fool. It was bad enough that Johnny had me licked. I wished I'd never told him I had a secret plan. Now he was laughing at me, and that hurt worst of all.

My mood wasn't improved by the fact that I was stuck visiting Mr. Rotten. But soon that would be the only job I'd have, so I wasn't about to give it up.

"You here again?" he grunted as he opened the door.

"Yes, I am," I said. "And I'll be here tomorrow, and the day after tomorrow and next week and the week after that. You might as well get used to the idea."

"Promises, promises," Mr. Rotten said. "I'll get my coat. We'll go for a walk."

"Fine," I said, even though it wasn't.

Mr. Rotten came out a moment later, wearing his

coat and carrying his cane. He walked down the steps carefully, since they'd iced over a bit.

"Lousy ice," he said, glaring at me.

"The ice isn't my fault," I told him.

"Lousy ice, lousy weather," he continued. "Snow and ice. It stinks."

"Does it make your bones hurt?" I asked. Cold weather made my grandmother's bones hurt, which was why she spent winters in Florida.

"My bones don't hurt," Mr. Rotten replied. "What do you take me for, one of those old guys whose bones hurt?"

"I was just trying to be polite," I said. "I'm glad your bones don't hurt."

"Liar," Mr. Rotten growled. "You wish my bones hurt, don't you? Admit it."

"I will not admit it," I said, "because it wouldn't be true." If his bones did hurt, his mood would only be worse. I didn't think I could stand a worse Mr. Rotten.

"Only good thing about winter is the short days," Mr. Rotten said, as we started walking around the block. "Short days mean longer nights."

"You like that?" I asked.

"Sure," Mr. Rotten said. "More time for trouble in the dark. You like trouble?"

"Not especially," I said. "What kind of trouble?"

"Oh, you know," Mr. Rotten said. "Just trouble."

I had never seen the inside of Mr. Rotten's house, and I shivered with relief. He probably kept his shotguns and axes in his refrigerator and stored dead bodies in the dining room.

"Look at those lousy kids," Mr. Rotten said, pointing

at a couple of little kids building a snowman. "Sure they're having a good time now, but they'll pay with pain and suffering. Why should they be different?"

' "I agree," I said. I'd felt my share of pain and suffering lately, and was perfectly willing to believe it had all been caused by good times I'd had when I was six.

"You agree?" Mr. Rotten asked.

"Sure," I replied. "There's too much pain and suffering in this world."

"I never said there's too much," Mr. Rotten declared. "Just that nobody's immune."

"I know someone who's immune," I told him.

"No such animal," Mr. Rotten said. "Pain and suffering strikes us all. Take my word for it."

"If you say so," I said. What I needed was a way to take some of my pain and suffering and give it to Johnny, who so richly deserved it.

And then I remembered what Dad had said about going to experts for advice. I needed advice on how to stop Johnny, and here I was walking with the nastiest man I ever hoped to meet. If anybody could come up with a scheme to stop Johnny, it was bound to be Mr. Rotten.

"I need your help," I said, almost without thinking.

"Forget it," Mr. Rotten said. "I'm not going to help you. I pay you to help me, remember?"

"Don't say no so fast," I told him. "I think you'll like this."

"I don't like anything," Mr. Rotten grumbled.

"I know that," I said. "Just listen to my problem, and see what you think." So I told him about Johnny and how I needed a way to stop him.

Mr. Rotten and I kept walking as I talked. Even if he didn't come up with a solution, this was still better than having to listen to him all the time. I wondered if I could come up with a new problem every day for his amusement.

"That's a rough one," Mr. Rotten said. We were almost at his door, so I doubted he would be able to come up with something. And I certainly wasn't about to go into his house while he thought. He probably had the remains of enterprising kids scattered all over his hallways.

"If you can't think of anything, that's okay," I told him. "My father hasn't been able to think of anything either, except to negotiate."

"That's because he's a lawyer," Mr. Rotten replied. "Lawyers only know talk. They don't know action."

"And we need action?" I asked him.

"You sure need something," he said. "I guess your parents won't let you hurt this kid. No violence, right?"

"Right," I said. "Besides, even if they would let me, I'd lose. Johnny's a lot bigger than I am, and much meaner, too."

"But you have me," Mr. Rotten said. "You've come to the right person."

I held my breath. Maybe Mr. Rotten would come up with a plan. Everybody was good for something. Mr. Rotten was probably the best bad person in the world. That should be good for a lot.

"What you need is to do something so mean, so nasty that this kid will decide he never wants to shovel snow again," Mr. Rotten said.

"That would be ideal," I agreed.

"But it probably would be impossible," Mr. Rotten continued. "Unless you can break his kneecaps, which I gather you can't."

"Right," I said.

"So the next best thing is to get all his friends to quit working for him," Mr. Rotten said.

"You know, you're right," I said.

"Of course I am," Mr. Rotten said.

"Maybe I could break *their* kneecaps," I said.

"You think so?" Mr. Rotten asked.

I shook my head.

"Well, then, you have to do something that's going to make all Johnny's friends quit," Mr. Rotten said. "Have Johnny get them a job that works their butts off, and then see to it they don't get paid."

"But how can I do that?" I asked. We were standing outside Mr. Rotten's door, and I was terrified that he wouldn't tell me what to do or, worse yet, that he would invite me inside his house of torture.

"You could steal the money," Mr. Rotten suggested.

"I don't think so," I said.

"Then it's up to you to think of something," he said. "I can't do all your work for you." He unlocked his front door, walked inside, and slammed the door in my face.

I stared at the door for a moment, and then I kicked it in frustration. To my surprise, Mr. Rotten opened it. "You still here?" he asked.

"I need your help," I said.

"You need a job that Johnny's going to think pays but doesn't," Mr. Rotten said.

"You're right," I said, and suddenly I felt like singing. "And I know just the job that will do it!"

Chapter

10

The first step in stopping Johnny was coaching Carol and Lisa to make sure they knew their lines.

"Say it with conviction," I told them, as they rehearsed in my bedroom Sunday afternoon. "But casually."

"Casually but with conviction," Carol said. "You want everything, Janie."

"Kid Power depends on this," I reminded her.

"All right," Carol said. "Oh, Lisa, there you are. I'm glad I found you."

"What's up?" Lisa asked, just the way I'd coached her.

"Janie got Mrs. Dell to agree to let Kid Power shovel her walk," Carol said, casually, but with conviction. "The money is unbelievable, too. Would you believe twenty-five?"

This was very important to me. I didn't want to actually lie about the amount, but it was essential that Johnny think it was a lot of money. So I just had Carol forget to say "cents." If Johnny assumed it was dollars, that was his problem.

"Wow," Lisa replied. "But that's such a big job. It'll take at least four kids to shovel it."

"We want you to be one of them," Carol said. "Are you willing?"

"For that kind of money? Sure," Lisa said.

"Perfect," I declared. "Now, make sure to say all that when Johnny is listening, but act as if you don't see him."

"We understand," Carol said, but just to be on the safe side, I had them go over their lines again.

I couldn't be there when Carol and Lisa staged their scene, because it was important that Johnny think I didn't know he'd heard. The next day, I had to take Carol's word for it that everything had gone according to plan.

"It was better than that," Carol assured me. "Two of Johnny's friends were standing with him. The three of them huddled together as soon as Lisa and I stopped talking."

Step two involved gathering all of Kid Power's snow shovelers for a meeting at my house. Carol was a big help there, also, making phone calls to all the kids, and rounding them up so that I could tell everybody what was happening.

"It's absolutely vital that you all go out and shovel your assigned walks as soon as it stops snowing next time," I told them. "The sooner you get to your jobs, the fewer jobs Johnny and his friends will be able to steal. Now, we're hoping that once they see that the walks are being shoveled by Kid Power, they'll go over to Mrs. Dell's and shovel there. But you've got to start shoveling as early as possible. All right?"

"All right!" everybody shouted.

"Carol's going to call each and every one of you as soon as it stops snowing next time," I said. "So don't think we're just checking up on you. The future of Kid Power is dependent on all of you."

"Don't worry, Janie," Ted called out. "You can count on us."

I had the feeling I could, too. And that made me feel very good indeed.

The next step, of course, was up to the weather. I wanted to have snow-removal drills, but Carol vetoed that as being obsessive.

"Nobody likes to look dumb," she pointed out to me. "And it's going to look real dumb to be out on the streets shoveling imaginary snow."

So I bit my nails, waiting for the snow to fall.

I wasn't the only nail biter in the family that week. My mother was waiting to hear from Mayor Rhazhnophski.

"I've called her twice," she moaned at supper. "You'd think she'd return my calls, just to get me off her back."

"She's probably very busy," Dad said. "Give her another week, and then call again."

"I've got to hear soon," Mom said. "If Something Extra is going to put on a successful winter carnival in January, we'll need some time to arrange things."

"So you'll have it in February," Dad said. "There's a lot of winter left, unfortunately."

"Don't say anything against winter," I said. "We need more winter, not less."

"That's a little excessive," Mom said. "Oh, I hope Mayor Rhazhnophski calls me soon."

"I hope it snows soon," I chimed in.

"I hope you shut up soon," Carol said. "Sorry. Force of habit."

So I smiled at her. We really had been getting along better now that we were working together.

In fact, it was Carol who first pointed out to me that it was snowing. It was on a Thursday, just three days after Lisa and Carol had staged the scene for Johnny. The flakes were falling bigger and heavier and more wonderfully than I could have imagined.

"Three snowfalls in less than a month," Mom said, staring at the snow falling in the glow of the streetlight. "And this looks as if it's going to be a real killer."

"It looks like four inches already," Dad said. "And it just started. I'll turn the radio on for a report."

I kept my fingers crossed. We needed lots of snow, but more important, we needed it to keep snowing all night long. I wouldn't have put it past Johnny to go shoveling at midnight just to undercut me. And no matter how willing my friends were to save Kid Power, I couldn't ask them to go out in the middle of the night to shovel.

Dad fiddled with the radio until he found a station that gave the local weather report. "Twelve to eighteen inches," the weather forecaster declared. "The snow is expected to end sometime late tomorrow morning."

"This is it!" I shouted, and soon Carol and I were dancing around the living room.

I didn't get very much sleep that night. As soon as I'd fall off to sleep, I'd start dreaming about snow, and that would wake me up. I got out of bed at least three times during the night to check on the snow. It kept falling softly and steadily.

I gave up trying to sleep at six, and dressed and made myself breakfast. It was bound to be a long morning, and I wasn't going to make the no-breakfast mistake again. Whatever happened, I wanted to be well fed.

Carol joined me and made herself a bowl of cereal and milk. We watched out the kitchen window as the snow kept falling. "I think it's lightening up," she said. "It should be over in about an hour."

"Do you think our plan is going to work?" I asked her.

"I sure hope so," Carol said. "Because I don't know what other kind of scheme you're going to come up with if it doesn't."

Mom walked into the kitchen still in her robe. It was a good morning to be lazy in. "Your father is still sleeping," she said. "There's no point in his even trying to drive to the office today."

"I guess Carol and I are going to be the only ones working today," I said.

"It looks that way," Mom said. "Oh, well, maybe Mayor Rhazhnophski will spend the day catching up with her reading."

"The snow is definitely slowing down," Carol said. "I'm going to start making phone calls."

"I'm going over to Herm's to start shoveling," I said.

"Do that," Mom said. "And take care of your other clients, too. But don't rush to do our walk. Check up on your other concerns first, if you want."

"Thanks, Mom," I said, and got up to hug her. Then I put on my boots and my heavy coat and my gloves and made my way outside to start shoveling.

It wasn't easy. Just getting to Herm's house was a struggle, since most of the people hadn't cleaned their walks yet. It took me ten minutes to get to the end of the block, and another ten to make it to Herm's.

Herm was nowhere to be seen, which was fine with me. There was no way I was going to be able to rush through the job this morning. The snow was very heavy, and there was well over a foot of it. I made a solemn vow as I pushed, groaned, and grunted, that I would start lifting weights that weekend.

After a while, I developed a rhythm, which included taking an occasional breather. I also started singing. Not too loudly, but enough so I was distracted from the pain by trying to remember words to songs I half knew.

And in spite of the cold and the way my arms and back were aching, I was having a good time. The snow had pretty much stopped, but I was still the only person out shoveling. That made me feel good, like a pioneer. I pretended I was a pioneer woman, shoveling out her home on the prairie. I wondered if Elvira Butsworth had ever shoveled snow.

The snowplow drove by and pushed the snow to the side of the street, where it blocked the driveway. But I hadn't started shoveling there yet, so I didn't mind as much as I would have if I'd already dug it out. Instead, I shoveled and grunted and sang "She Works Hard for the Money" and other prairie snow-shoveling songs.

After what felt like forever, I was satisfied with my job. I walked up to Gert's door and rang the bell.

"You did a wonderful job!" Gert exclaimed as she looked around. "Herm, come see the job Janie did."

So Herm checked it out, too. "Good job," he said. "Much better than I used to do."

"I know your fee is three fifty," Gert said. "But you were so prompt this morning and worked so hard that I want you to take five dollars."

"Just this once," I said, taking the money.

"Absolutely," Gert declared. "Thank you again, Janie."

"Thank you," I said, and made my way to Gail's house. It was a little easier getting around now, since other people had begun to shovel.

It took me a long time to shovel Gail's walk, and I was already tired of singing, so I spent my time there worrying about how the other kids were doing. Worrying was very time-consuming, and it helped keep my mind off my pain. There had to be easier ways of making a fortune, I decided. Maybe my computer would be able to tell me how.

"I'd love to pay you a little extra," Gail said, as she handed me my three fifty. "But money is so tight."

"That's okay," I said.

"Would you like some cookies?" she asked. "I baked some this morning, so they're still warm."

"That sounds great," I told her, and devoured the cookies as soon as she handed them to me. Snow shoveling really made me hungry, and Gail's cookies were the best I'd ever eaten. "Do you bake a lot?" I asked her.

"As often as I can afford to," Gail said.

"You should call my mother," I said, and then I explained to her about Something Extra. There had to be room in the organization for somebody who baked as well as Gail did.

"Thank you," Gail said, when I gave her our number. "I'd love to get some part-time work that I could do at home. I'll call your mother this afternoon."

That made me feel a lot better, and I didn't turn down Gail's offer of a couple of extra cookies for the road, either. I ate them as I walked over to Mrs. Edwards's house. About a third of the houses had been dug out already, and that made walking and eating cookies possible. Even so, I had to climb over some huge mounds of snow to get there.

I was never so happy as when I realized I only had to shovel Mrs. Edwards's walk, and didn't have to do her driveway. I didn't sing, and I didn't worry. I just shoveled as fast as I could.

Mrs. Edwards paid me and offered to make me a cup of hot chocolate. Ordinarily I would have been happy to take her up on it, but I wanted to go to Mrs. Dell's house and see what was happening.

It was quite a walk from Mrs. Edwards's to Mrs. Dell's, but I plowed ahead, terrified of what I might see. Maybe Mrs. Dell would be so impressed with Johnny's work that she really would pay him twenty-five dollars. She might even adopt him. Or maybe Johnny had seen through the trick and was stealing work from Kid Power again. All the worrying I hadn't been doing at Mrs. Edwards's I did on my walk.

When I got to Mrs. Dell's, I found Carol and Lisa crouched behind some shrubs. I squatted down next to them.

"They've been shoveling for half an hour," Lisa whispered to me. "See? All four of them."

"I only got here a few minutes ago," Carol whispered. "I walked over to check up on some of the other kids' jobs, and Johnny and his crowd hadn't done any of them. I knew they came here first, and this is all they've done today."

I watched silently as the boys worked. My body ached, and it was hard not to shiver from cold and exhaustion, but I was determined to stay there and watch the payoff.

It took another ten minutes before the boys were finished. They'd done a magnificent job. Mrs. Dell was bound to be satisfied. I just hoped she was satisfied but cheap.

Johnny rang the doorbell, and Mrs. Dell came to the door. I couldn't hear what was being said, but it was easy to see she paid him with a coin. And then she went inside, while Johnny remained at her opened door.

"She's going to give him more money," Lisa moaned. "Oh, no, I can't stand it."

"It's okay," I said. "Even if she does pay him more, it's still kept them from shoveling the Kid Power walks."

But when Mrs. Dell reappeared in the doorway, she only handed Johnny more coins.

We could hear Johnny's shriek loud and clear. "Twenty-eight cents!" he screamed. "You gave me a quarter and three pennies!"

"I don't believe it," Carol whispered. "She gave him pennies! She gave him twenty-eight cents, so he could divide it equally with his friends."

"What's going on?" one of Johnny's friends asked, and soon they were all gathered around Johnny, who showed them the twenty-eight cents. Mrs. Dell had slammed the door shut as soon as Johnny began screaming, and it was a good thing, too. She probably had never heard most of the words Johnny's friends were using.

"You told us we were going to get twenty-five dollars," one of his friends shouted. "You're an idiot, Johnny. I'm not going to work for you anymore."

"Me neither," one of the other boys said.

"Same here," the third boy said. "I can do better working for Kid Power."

That was when Johnny really started screaming. I'd never seen anybody quite that shade of purple before.

"I think we should get out of here," Carol said, and it seemed like good advice, so we ran as fast as we could. Thanks to the job Johnny and his friends had done, it was no problem making a fast getaway.

"I have a stop to make before I go home," I told Carol and Lisa. "Tell Mom I'll be back for lunch."

"All right," Carol said. "Lisa, you want to come home with me and wait for Janie?"

"I'd like that," Lisa said, so I watched as they walked away. I turned left at the corner and made my way to Mr. Rotten's house.

"It worked!" I cried, as soon as he opened the door. "Our plan worked!"

"Yippee!" Mr. Rotten shouted, and then he hugged me. "I knew we could do it."

"I never could have without your help," I told him. "Thank you so much, Mr. Ro . . ."

"Rhazhnophski," he said, pronouncing it slowly.

"Rhazhnophski?" I said. "Like the mayor?"

"She's my daughter-in-law," Mr. Rotten said. "You want to meet her? She's right inside."

"Sure," I said, and followed Mr. Rotten into his living room. It turned out to be a very pretty room, with no skulls in it at all.

"So you're Janie," a woman said. She was sitting on the living room sofa, sipping a cup of coffee. "My father-in-law talks about you all the time."

"I talk about him a lot, too," I said.

"Our plan worked," Mr. Rotten told the mayor. "You know, the plan I was telling you about."

"That's great," the mayor said. "You must be very happy, Janie."

"I am," I said. "But there's something that would make me even happier."

"And what's that?" Mayor Rhazhnophski asked.

"My mother sent you a proposal," I said. "For a winter festival in honor of Elvira Butsworth."

"Oh, yes, that," the mayor said. "I keep meaning to read it, but things have been so hectic."

"Do you think you could read it today?" I asked her. "It would mean so much to my mother."

Mayor Rhazhnophski smiled. "I think I can manage that," she said. "Today is a perfect day to read about winter festivals."

"See!" Mr. Rotten chortled. "I told you everybody is out for number one!"

"Number one and her mother," I said, but I giggled along with him. Today, even Mr. Rotten wasn't really rotten.

Chapter 11

It was a long shot, but I couldn't think of anything else to try.

"I'll help you, Mom," I said Monday morning. "You have so much to do with the winter carnival. I'll help."

Of course it didn't work. "You have school today," Mom replied. "School is just a little more important than planning for the winter carnival, Janie."

I sighed. The weekend had just zipped by, ever since Mom had heard from Mayor Rhazhnophski that the project was fine with her. The city council had to approve it officially, but Mom had decided to get things organized while she was waiting for the council's decision. So she'd made a thousand phone calls and held a hundred conferences with the Something Extra people as well as with Dad, Carol, and me. I'd never seen her so excited. But my hopes that she was excited enough to forget that Monday was a school day had just been shot down.

"Scared of running into Johnny?" Carol asked me, as she walked past Mom and me.

I nodded.

"You're going to have to face Johnny sometime," Mom pointed out. "It might as well be now. He's had a weekend to cool off, after all. That should be a help."

"Just remember to hold your ground," Dad said, pouring himself a cup of coffee. "Be firm, but not obnoxious."

"Sure," I said, because there wasn't anything else I could say to parents. Either Johnny was going to kill me or he wasn't, and I wouldn't know for sure until after I'd spoken to him. I just hoped he'd vote not to kill me. The shock to my parents might be too great otherwise.

"Want me to stick around?" Carol asked as we approached the school.

"Don't bother," I said. I didn't think my parents would be able to stand the shock of losing both their daughters. So Carol walked over to her friends, and I walked into the building and went straight to my locker.

"Hey, Golden."

There was no point in not turning around, so I did. There was Johnny, big, mean, and probably armed.

"Yeah, Richards," I said, trying to snarl.

"We got some talking to do," Johnny said.

"You better believe it," I said. "Lunch. My table."

"Right," Johnny said.

"Right," I said, my heart pounding. I was still alive. I'd stay alive at least until lunch. My world looked brighter already.

I considered surrounding myself with my friends at lunch, but I decided that wouldn't be fair to Johnny, who had lost all his friends, after all, thanks to me. Two of them had called that weekend to see about working for Kid Power, but I'd had Carol put them off. Still, if Johnny was going to be alone, I should be, too. So I told my friends to start lunch without me, and I found a corner table that was empty.

Johnny joined me almost immediately, but I'd already started eating my sandwich. Let him watch me chew. Maybe he'd learn some table manners.

"You think you're pretty smart, don't you?" Johnny said, as he sat down. He unwrapped his sandwich, which was tuna salad again. There was something about Johnny that made me vow never to eat tuna fish again.

"I told you I had ways," I reminded him.

"Yeah, but I figured you were bluffing," Johnny replied. "Who would have thought you really did have ways?"

"Next time maybe you'll respect me a little more," I said. "As much as I respect you."

"You don't respect me," Johnny said. "Maybe you're scared of me, but you don't respect me."

"Sure, I respect you," I said. "You're the best snow shoveler I've ever seen. You do beautiful work. A person could eat off a sidewalk you've shoveled." Probably with better table manners, too.

"I am good," Johnny said. "It comes from being strong."

"I'd like to be that strong," I said. "I was going to start lifting weights over the weekend, but I ached too much. Maybe this weekend."

"Don't do too much at first," Johnny said. "You got to build up gradually, or else you'll strain yourself."

"I'll remember that," I said. "Thank you."

"You're welcome," he replied. "Now what are we going to do?"

"We're going to compete with each other," I told him. "I don't want to put you out of business. I mean, I'd love to put you out of business, but your work is too good. I'll never be able to drive you out."

"What's going to stop me from driving *you* out?" Johnny asked, sounding like the miserable old Johnny again.

"I have ways, Johnny," I said, giving him my best smile. "Did you spend your seven cents all at once, or did you spread it around?"

Johnny glowered for a moment, but then he grinned. "Okay," he said. "You don't drive me out, I don't drive you out. Now, what about my friends?"

"What about them?" I asked.

"They joining Kid Power?" he asked, and I could see that he really cared.

I'd thought a lot about that over the weekend. On the one hand, they'd be a big asset to Kid Power, since they were very good at shoveling. And it would be nice to have that little triumph over Johnny. But on the other hand, I didn't want to have anything more to do with them than I absolutely had to. And I would hate it if Lisa and Margie and Ted left Kid Power to join up with Johnny.

"Kid Power has enough members right now," I replied. "We're not taking anybody new on."

"So they can stay with me?" Johnny asked.

"If you can get them back, they're yours," I said. "Whatever happens, though, they won't be joining Kid Power."

"This compromising stuff is okay," Johnny declared, taking a huge bite out of his sandwich to show his pleasure.

"Hold on one second," I said. "We haven't begun compromising yet."

"Yeah, Golden?" Johnny asked, giving me a look that would have demolished me a few minutes earlier. I was feeling tougher than that now, though.

"Yeah, Richards," I said. "We've got to get some things settled now, once and for all."

"Settle," Johnny said, putting his sandwich down.

"You don't ever claim to be Kid Power again," I said. "You don't steal our jobs from us. Not you, not your friends. You shovel your walks and leave our walks to us. If I hear from just one kid that you or your friends treaded on our turf, all deals are off."

Johnny looked me over. "I like you, Golden," he declared. "You're tough, you know that? You look like a real nothing, but there's something to you."

"I'm glad you like me, Johnny," I told him, "but don't think that means I won't do what I have to to keep Kid Power alive."

Johnny raised his hands in surrender. "Fair's fair," he said. "You shovel your turf, I shovel mine."

"You got it," I said, and held out my hand. Johnny took it, and we shook on the deal. And then we spent the rest of lunch discussing muscle-building techniques.

It felt so good to have that problem out of the way that I raced home after school and volunteered all over again to help Mom with the winter carnival. I didn't have to bother. Mom had every intention of drafting me, Carol, and Dad into helping, whether we wanted to or not.

Fortunately, there was lots of time to help during Christmas vacation. And we had plenty to keep us busy, especially after the city council officially approved the

Elvira Butsworth Winter Carnival. The minute that happened, Mom put ads in the paper and held a press conference. From then on, we didn't have a quiet moment in the house. Dad, Carol, and I worked at our regular jobs, but every spare moment we had we spent helping out with the carnival. We helped distribute posters, and send out invitations, and come up with ideas for events. Meanwhile Mom was organizing all the Something Extra people to cook and bake and chauffeur and design posters and do whatever else had to be done.

There was a lot of work, but we all enjoyed doing it, and everybody cooperated. Even the weather behaved itself. After all those early snowstorms, we'd only had one four-inch snowfall right after Christmas. And then, two days before the festival, just as Mom was starting to get desperate, we got ten inches. Which gave Kid Power and Johnny and his friends plenty to shovel.

The weather for the carnival was perfect, too. The temperature was around thirty (which by that point in January felt warm), there were bright sunny skies, and the leftover snow from the storm was still white and clean. The pond in Butsworth Park, where the festival was being held, was frozen solid, and the free-skating competition was being fiercely fought as I took a break from the Something Extra booth.

We all took turns there, including Dad, handing out literature about Something Extra and explaining what it was and why it had decided to throw Elvira Butsworth a party. Mom couldn't spend too much time in the booth, since she was busy supervising the festival, and being interviewed by the papers and radio and TV. I was interviewed on TV, too, and threw in a plug for Kid Power.

Everybody I knew was at the carnival, even Mrs. Edwards. She was talking with Mr. Rotten, and judging from the way she was shaking her head, he was telling her his philosophy of life. But even if Mrs. Edwards was disagreeing with what he said, she was enjoying arguing with him. I could tell that from the way her eyes sparkled.

Everything was sparkly that day. The sun reflected brightly off the snow, and the sky turned the pond to an icy blue. People were walking around, eating cookies that Gail had baked, and drinking hot chocolate that Something Extra had provided, and admiring the different snow people that the different school teams had sculpted. Mayor Rhazhnophski was the judge, and she was examining each one carefully while a photographer snapped pictures.

Margie had organized a sled-pulling service for Kid Power at Christmas. Kid Power kids hired themselves out to pull younger kids around on their new sleds. It was a real back-saver for parents and had proved to be pretty successful. The service was hard at work at the festival, with a half dozen Kid Power members pulling squealing kids around. Other kids were building a town of miniature snow people; Lisa and her little brother Stevie were busy there.

After the figure-skating contest came speed-skating races, and then to end it all there was going to be a snowbank tug-of-war. Whoever lost was going to end up in a huge snowbank. I'd signed up to be on one of the teams, and I sure hoped I wouldn't be on the losing side. But I had been working on building my muscles, and that should help. The last snowstorm hadn't hurt my back and arms nearly as much as the earlier ones had.

The festival was in full swing as I walked around, enjoying all I was seeing. Gail's people were working on the little snowpeople town. Lisa's brother had walked away from that and, along with a dozen other kids, was trying to knock over bottles with snowballs. Mayor Rhazhnophski had just completed her judging and was hanging ribbons on the winning snow sculptures.

I edged over to my mother, who was talking with a reporter. The reporter was taking down everything she said in a notebook. It wasn't easy for the reporter to hold on to the pen with her gloves on, so every time she dropped the pen, I bent down and picked it up for her.

"It turns out that Elvira Butsworth's birthday is in July," Mom was saying. "So I'm hoping the mayor and the city council will decide to hold a summer festival in her honor this year."

"Will Something Extra do the organizing?" the reporter asked.

"If we're asked," Mom said. "We've certainly had a wonderful time organizing this carnival. Of course, Something Extra does a lot more than organize town fairs. One of the more interesting developments for Something Extra is that three different civic groups have approached us about helping them set up their annual meetings. We're organizing a Valentine's Day dinner dance for one group, and we plan to arrange a Mardi Gras party for another."

"So Something Extra is flourishing?" the reporter asked, dropping her pen again. I picked it up one last time, and left before hearing Mom give another glowing answer. She'd been so excited about Something Extra the past few weeks it had been almost scary.

"See, Janie?" Carol had said to me one night after we'd had to listen to Mom go on and on all through supper. "That's what you used to be like with Kid Power. Before you got smart and hired me, that is."

"I was never that bad," I said, but Mom, Dad, and Carol all said "Oh, yes, you were" so fast that I had to admit I probably had been.

I walked over to Herm and Gert, who were talking to one of the Something Extra people about gourmet cooking for people on low sodium diets. "See this girl?" Gert said, giving me a hug. "This girl is keeping my husband alive."

"I have lots of help," I said. "Herm is the biggest help of all."

"Easiest job I've ever had," Herm said. "All I have to do is sleep late and sit back and watch while this girl does all the hard work for me."

"It's my pleasure," I told them. It was, too.

"Come on, everybody!" Mayor Rhazhnophski shouted into the microphone. "It's time for the tug-of-war."

"You're going to have to tug for me today, Janie," Herm said. "Gert won't let me."

Gert laughed. "Janie will do you proud," she said. "Go on, honey, and be careful. You don't want to end up in a snowbank."

"You're right about that," I said, and ran off to join my team.

"Hey, Golden!"

"Yeah, Richards?" I replied.

"Better watch it," he shouted. "I'm on the other team."

"So what else is new?" I said. "But you're the one who'd better be careful."

"Right," he said. "You have ways."

"Not only do I have ways," I told him. "I have muscles, too."

We were both laughing when we got to the tug-of-war. I grabbed my section of rope, happy to be sandwiched between my father and Carol. If our team lost, there'd be three cold, wet Goldens to be taken care of.

"Don't forget to pull," Carol told me. "Pull as hard as you can."

"I intend to," I replied. And I did, too. I wasn't just pulling for me, or even for the Golden family. I was pulling for Something Extra and for Elvira Butsworth, and Mr. Rotten, and Herm and Gert, and Mrs. Edwards, and Gail, and Gail's kids, and Lisa, and my school, and even for Johnny. But mostly I was pulling for Kid Power and its future.

"Come on, everybody!" I shouted. "Let's pull together."

And we did.

About the Author

SUSAN BETH PFEFFER is a native New Yorker. She was graduated from New York University with a B.A. in Television, Motion Pictures, and Radio. She has written many books for young readers and young adults, including *Starting with Melodie, Kid Power, The Friendship Pact,* and *Truth or Dare,* available as Apple Paperbacks.

APPLE® PAPERBACKS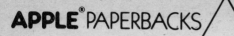

Delicious Reading!

NEW APPLE® TITLES $2.50 each

☐ FM 40382-6 **Oh Honestly, Angela!** Nancy K. Robinson
☐ FM 40305-2 **Veronica the Show-Off** Nancy K. Robinson
☐ FM 33662-2 **DeDe Takes Charge!** Johanna Hurwitz
☐ FM 40180-7 **Sixth Grade Can Really Kill You** Barthe DeClements
☐ FM 40874-7 **Stage Fright** Ann M. Martin
☐ FM 40513-6 **Witch Lady Mystery** Carol Beach York
☐ FM 40452-0 **Ghosts Who Went to School** Judith Spearing
☐ FM 33946-X **Swimmer** Harriet May Savitz
☐ FM 40406-7 **Underdog** Marilyn Sachs

BEST-SELLING APPLE® TITLES

☐ FM 40725-2 **Nothing's Fair in Fifth Grade** Barthe DeClements
☐ FM 40466-0 **The Cybil War** Betsy Byars
☐ FM 40529-2 **Amy and Laura** Marilyn Sachs
☐ FM 40950-6 **The Girl with the Silver Eyes** Willo Davis Roberts
☐ FM 40755-4 **Ghosts Beneath Our Feet** Betty Ren Wright
☐ FM 40605-1 **Help! I'm a Prisoner in the Library** Eth Clifford
☐ FM 40724-4 **Katie's Baby-sitting Job** Martha Tolles
☐ FM 40607-8 **Secrets in the Attic** Carol Beach York
☐ FM 40534-9 **This Can't Be Happening at Macdonald Hall!**
Gordon Korman
☐ FM 40687-6 **Just Tell Me When We're Dead!** Eth Clifford